CARESS OF FUR

3xtasy Lake 1

Corinne Davies

MENAGE EVERLASTING

Siren Publishing, Inc.
www.SirenPublishing.com

A SIREN PUBLISHING BOOK
IMPRINT: Ménage Everlasting

CARESS OF FUR
Copyright © 2011 by Corinne Davies

ISBN-10: 1-61034-503-7
ISBN-13: 978-1-61034-503-3

First Printing: March 2011

Cover design by *Les Byerley*
All cover art and logo copyright © 2011 by Siren Publishing, Inc.

ALL RIGHTS RESERVED: This literary work may not be reproduced or transmitted in any form or by any means, including electronic or photographic reproduction, in whole or in part, without express written permission.

All characters and events in this book are fictitious. Any resemblance to actual persons living or dead is strictly coincidental.

Printed in the U.S.A.

PUBLISHER
Siren Publishing, Inc.
www.SirenPublishing.com

DEDICATION

For my friend and kindred spirit, Roszika.

And, Miss Turner, this is for you and the fun times we shared. I miss you guys.

CARESS OF FUR

3xtasy Lake 1

CORINNE DAVIES
Copyright © 2011

Chapter One

Mai lay on her living room floor staring at the crack snaking across the old plaster on her ceiling. The original ceilings were one of the reasons she purchased this apartment. A true artisan had created the intricate swirls and designs. Too bad the building hadn't been as well. The crack was an obvious result of the building setting over the last fifty years, and the heartbreaking part was she didn't have the money to fix it.

Every penny she earned from her website designs went into upgrading her computer and programs so that she could handle bigger and better. The demand for professional websites increased in recent years, but then so did the suppliers and the hackers. She needed to stay one step ahead of the competition and the criminals. Which meant she spent every waking moment she could in front of the computer. Not that it mattered at the moment, since one of her biggest clients decided to go with a big fancy marketing company with an army of techs at their disposal. She really couldn't afford to lose them and pay her bills.

Her phone rang, but Mai ignored it. They could leave a message. She wasn't finished with her own pity party. When her old-fashioned answering machine picked up, she heard her best friend, really her only friend's voice. "Mai I know your there. You better pick up or I'm coming over. I'll play on your computer again…"

Mai followed a few simple but precise rules in her life.

1. Never let Stephanie touch her computer.

2. Never shop for groceries after seven a.m.

3. Unlike people, except for Stephanie, computers never lie.

Succumbing to the inevitable, she grabbed her phone. "Hey, Steph, what's up?"

"Brodie will be picking you up at five thirty for dinner."

Mai's stomach cramped up at the thought of leaving her apartment. She had things to do. First off, she needed to pick up a new client, even through the idea of going out and cold calling companies made her heart race and her palms sweat. "Steph, I'm swamped. I can't come for dinner tonight."

"You always say that, and you need to get out. It's not a request. I'm being bossy here."

"I get out lots."

"Oh yeah, where? I dare you to name four places."

"I went grocery shopping, to the bank, saw a movie, and um…" Mai scrambled to come up with fourth errand. "I stopped into Victoria's Secret and picked up a few things."

"Mai, you remember the movie with Sandra Bullock? The one where no one knows her because she does everything on the computer? You're turning into Sandra Bullock's character."

"I am not. I hate pizza."

She could hear the frustration in her friend's voice and wished that Steph could understand her fears. Going outside was becoming increasingly more difficult for her. Rationally, she knew this wasn't completely healthy, but she couldn't change right now.

Soon.

Soon. She would make changes in her life as soon as she could afford to.

"Mai, if you don't come to visit soon, Bella is going to start to forget her favorite Auntie."

"Bella's only three months old, Steph."

"Exactly my point. You need to come over. I can see it in her eyes. She misses you and wants you to visit more often. Come for dinner tonight. Brodie said he would be happy to pick you up."

"I know, and I'd love to but…" A heavy knock at her door sent her heart into her throat. Who would be knocking? No one came to visit her. "Um, Steph, I think I'll have to call you back." She whispered the words. Hopefully, who ever stood on the other side of her door would go away if they thought no one was home.

"No, it's okay I'll stay on the line." Stephanie continued to chatter as Mai snuck to the front door and looked through the peephole. An extraordinarily large man leaned back against the hallway and smirked at her, as she looked though the peephole.

"Dammit, Stephanie."

"Did I say five thirty? I meant that Brodie would be there in about five and a half minutes."

It felt like her heart jumped hard against her chest. A heart attack, maybe? Her stomach cramped, and a wave of nausea gripped her stomach. She wouldn't open the door. If she stayed quiet enough, maybe he would leave. She would come up with an excuse later when she could think straight. A quick look through the peephole demolished that plan. He waved his fingers at her and then tapped his watch. *Fuck!* Her heart slammed harder and a chill ran down her spine at the thought of leaving her home. "Damn, how does he do that?"

"Do what?"

"Know that I'm looking through the peephole. There is no way he heard me."

"I love my big bear, but he has talents that are beyond my explanation. Here's a crazy suggestion, let him in." Steph often referred to her husband as her big bear, and Mai could kind of see why. Broad-shouldered and barrel-chested, with black hair and a thick goatee, Brodie towered over her and Steph. His eyes were so dark they looked black. Mai thought he looked like a big, strong biker. Considering how delicate and ethereal her friend was, it amazed her that they ended up together. But, Brodie's rustic-looking outside hid a big ole soft heart of golden marshmallow.

"I can't do this, Stephie. I promise I'll come over tomorrow." She would take the subway, no a taxi. That way, she could tell the driver to pull over if she needed to get out.

"Mai, please come over. I made lasagna."

With those three words, she knew her fate. "Sneaky wench." She loved Steph's pasta. *Take a deep breath, Brodie's safe.* If the fears got too bad, then she would make an excuse to leave. "All right." She disconnected Stephanie's cheers. With no point in delaying the inevitable, Mai opened the door.

Brodie smiled warmly at her. "Let me guess, that's the love of my life on the phone?"

Mai returned the smile and reminded herself that she didn't need to panic around him. Brodie could easily keep her safe from any physical threat. Too bad he didn't know how to fix her emotional attacks. Now, if only she could get her heart rate to relax a bit and the humongous knot in her throat to relax.

"Um, Brodie."

He cut her off before she tried to make up another excuse. "Mai, I know that Stephanie talked you into this but, sweetheart, you need to get out more. It's not healthy staying in your apartment all the time."

"I know but..." Mai could feel the familiar rise of panic in her system. The more she tried to fight it, the more control it had over her.

Brodie held out his large hand. "Okay, how about this? You come with me, and I promise to keep you safe. If at any time you want to turn around and go home, we will go."

"Really?"

"Honestly." His large hand swallowed hers. Mai always tried very hard to hide her feelings and didn't want anyone around her to know when she lost control and panicked. Somehow, Brodie always knew when she felt scared.

"I wouldn't want to upset Stephanie if I didn't show up."

He patted her shoulder with his free hand. "Let me worry about Stephanie. She loves you and would understand. I swear, Mai. I'll bring you straight back here the moment you need to, I promise."

If only another man existed out there for her. One as sweet at Steph's husband, but as her best friend liked to comment, Brodie was one of a kind.

* * * *

Gaspar stood at the glass window of his bedroom and looked out over the harbor. He loved the look of the Toronto skyline harbor at night. The city lights reflected off the water, a nighttime rainbow with the colorful way the lights on the CN Tower changed against the night sky.

He flipped his cell phone over in one hand waiting for the damn thing to go off. His brother, Vencel, would be home from work soon, and he had tickets to the Rock's opening game. Watching Toronto's professional lacrosse team was simply something to pass the time before hockey season started. Gaspar enjoyed the game, but Vencel's passion for hockey knew no boundaries. He'd been avidly following the Leaf's for a few decades now, making Gaspar wonder if his brother loved rooting for the underdog...or he caught this strange obsession Toronto had with their home team.

His phone beeped, and he glanced down at the screen.

@ACC. WTF R U.

"Asshole," he muttered and grabbed his shirt off the back of a chair and headed toward the door as he dialed his brother's number.

"I thought you were going to meet me here."

"Don't be bitchy. You only live a few blocks away. I'm hungry and wanted a couple sausages."

"I don't know how you eat that crap."

"Because I'm not as delicate as you."

"I'll show you delicate, puppy."

A low growl rumbled across the phone line making Gaspar laugh. "Be careful, you'll scare the humans."

"Are you on your way or am I going to the game without you?"

"I'm in the elevator. Give me a few minutes to get down the street, and I'll meet you by gate 23."

"See you in a couple."

As soon as Gaspar stepped out of his building, it felt like he walked into a wall of heat. Even now as the sun began to set, the city held on to the heat from the day. The air smelled stagnant and dirty, making him wish he was up north. He stepped to the curb and waved down a passing cab. His schedule was clear for the next few weeks, so why not head up there and get away from the smog and grim of the city?

The inside of the cab didn't smell any better, but at least it was air-conditioned. "ACC. Please." No sooner did they pull away from the curb did his phone go off. It was the ring programmed for his work number. "Hello."

"Um, hi." A hesitant female spoke on the other line, but in his line of work, rarely did women sound confident at first. "I'm looking for a Gas-par."

"Gosh-par." He corrected the pronunciation out of habit. "The *A* is soft, and you have him. How about your name?"

"Oh um...Stephanie." There was a slight hesitation, as if she debated on lying but chose not to. He could hear a lie in a woman's tone from a mile away.

"But I'm not phoning for me. I'm married, happily."

He could imagine the woman nodding her head as she spoke, followed by the rapid beat of her heart and the fact that she paced as she spoke to him. "That's great to hear. Did you want to hire me, Stephanie?"

"Yes." She hesitated again, her voice echoing with a distinct uncertainty as if she doubted her choice to call him.

"Okay, well you know what I do and that is why you called. So, if you don't need me for yourself, then who are you calling for?"

"My friend, Mai. Like the month but with an *I* not a *Y*."

"Pretty name."

"Oh she is, and she's my best friend. It's just that she really needs to go on a date, but if she thinks for one moment I set her up, she'll never show up."

"I have to tell you Stephanie, hiring me as a surprise rarely goes over well. I don't enjoy being put in that position."

"Oh, I see your point. But Mai sits in front of a computer all day. She's smart, but she needs to go out. You don't have to tell her what you do…I'm not hiring you for that. Really, you don't have to tell her. In fact, I would prefer if you don't."

"Then why not set her up on a normal blind date with someone you know? Why choose a stranger?"

"Because, Mai is the sweetest person in the universe, and I love her like a sister, but I need someone that can make her feel good about herself. You have lots of experience with women, right?"

About a century's worth or so… "Yes, I'm comfortable with what I do."

"That's what I figured. So you can make her feel good about herself. Build up her self-esteem, encourage her to perhaps start thinking about more than her RAMs and ROMs. I want to hire you as a dinner companion, not the other stuff."

Gaspar smiled at her decisive avoidance of the more intimate possibilities of his job. "You're a fascinating woman, Stephanie. You'll phone an escort to go on a blind date with your best friend but won't talk about sex."

He heard a strangled sound from the other end of the phone. "No, I don't talk about that with strangers. Except to tell you, I'm not hiring you to fall all over Mai and make her uncomfortable. I'll kick your ass myself if I have to."

Gaspar smiled at the heated threat. Whoever this Mai might be, she was lucky to have such a protective friend. "All right, Stephanie. I understand and promise to keep my hands to myself. When do you want us to meet?"

"You need to know that Mai is a nervous person. She didn't used to be, but I think all that radiation coming off her computer is throwing off her natural energies. A good dinner and conversation would do wonders for her."

Stephanie was starting to sound like a nutcase, and Gaspar wondered if this could be an elaborate setup or a crank call. "Okay, well, why don't you tell me when you want to set this up for?"

"Oh, I hear the car pulling up. Can I text you the details?"

"Absolutely. I'll need a couple day's notice, but then it should be fine."

"Thank you for being understanding, Gaspar."

"I look forward to hearing from you and meeting your friend, Mai."

Gaspar ended the call and wondered if he would hear anymore out of the woman. He often received calls that were more curiosity than an actual interest in hiring him.

He looked out the window at the traffic. Whenever the Air Canada Centre hosted an event, the traffic down here increased depending on the event in question. The lacrosse team playing didn't cause half the traffic headaches that a Maple Leafs hockey game brought, but it still remained incredibly busy down here.

The cab rounded the corner and stopped long enough for Gaspar to pay the man and then jump out. Vencel stood on the other side of the sidewalk, leaning against the wall, a sausage in one hand and a can of pop in the other. "Business is good?" His brother nodded to the phone still in Gaspar's hand.

"I could have too much if I wanted to, even after weeding out the crackpots, but lately I've been turning down anything more than a dinner request."

"Any particular reason?" Vencel levered himself off the wall and washed the last of the sausage down with the Coke.

"Boredom, I guess. Who knows? Maybe the stars will align and we'll find our mate."

Vencel grunted, acting as if the sausage in his hand was of more interest. "Come on, we have enough time for a couple beers before the game starts."

* * * *

Vencel knew finding a mate after all these years seemed unlikely. Even living in a city as big as Toronto, he felt their chances were slim to none. The city itself was filled with women of every shape and size but not the one meant for him and his brother. Who knew, maybe she did live here, but the odds of them finding her became smaller every year the population increased. What would happen when the urge to give in to their baser selves became too great to ignore? A city girl wouldn't be interested in living up in the wilderness they craved.

He had a lot of work in the city with all the condominiums being built, but he missed the forests of their homeland. He escaped the steel and window wonders of the city as often as he could. Deep down he wished they found a woman to complete them, but then how many women would be willing to be shared by brothers? Brothers that needed to run through the wilderness as wolves whenever the opportunity arose.

At times he wished they never left Hungary, but staying there under the threats of midnight raids and mass murder became impossible. The pack structure they grew up in dissolved during the war, mistrust and pointed fingers causing more deaths. It became one of those rare cases when safety was not in numbers. While many hid in the wilds in their animal form, many other families moved apart and tried to stay under the radar. When he and Gaspar escaped to this country, they never imagined that sixty-five years later, they would still be here. The fact they didn't age as fast as the humans forced them to move from their first North American home in the wilds of British Columbia. They needed to find a place to get lost in the crowd, and southern Ontario fit the bill. Now enough time had passed that they needed to start to think about the next place they would move to. The last thing they needed was a weak female dragging them down. As much as he wanted to deny it, his wolf craved his mate, but the man knew she would be nothing but trouble.

"Have you given more thought to what I spoke about the other day?"

"Yes, but I don't know if I want to permanently move up north already. Damn, Vencel, it's hard enough to find a woman in the city. What are we going to do up where the population is even scarcer?"

"We could move down to the States, but border crossings are getting harder and harder. For the time being, it's safer to stay in this country. Unless you want to move back to Hungary?"

"No, not really. I have been getting some pressure from the Hungarian packs for our return. Now that the wars are over we can live in safety there."

Vencel stared out at the field and sipped his beer. Going back to Hungary would be nice. They still had some family living, but with the invention of social networking websites, they could keep up with all the pack news. Canada had become a home to him, and he knew that Gaspar felt the same way. There wasn't much his brother felt that Vencel couldn't pick up on and vice-versa.

"I know you need to move on. We've been here for thirty years now and pretty soon people are going to notice that you haven't aged any."

"I actually got asked the other day if I was willing to share the identity of my surgeon." Vencel shook his head and took another swig of his beer. "I could go back to school and take up another line of work."

"Why don't you work with me? I could take care of twice the clients in half the time."

"No thank you. I learned the hard way that your chosen career isn't for me." He'd pinch-hit for Gaspar on a couple of occasions. Not that he disliked the experience, but he couldn't imagine doing it full time. He wanted a strong woman who could take care of herself and not rely on them. His brother, on the other hand, attracted and loved women who needed to be cared for.

Whistling, he cheered on the team and watched them toss a beauty of a goal. He didn't enjoy lacrosse as much as hockey, but it gave him something to watch in the off-season. "Leafs are going to start practicing in a couple weeks. Considering the drastic trades they made this year, I'm telling you, man. This year we are going to make it to the playoffs and walk away with the Cup."

Dropping down into his seat, he glanced over at his brother who didn't look as optimistic.

"You've said that every year for the last twenty-seven years."

"It's our time, this year, I'm telling you."

"Dude, the Leafs haven't recovered from loosing Sundin yet. How the hell do you think they are going to make it to the Stanley Cup?"

And with that comment, all concerns about moving or mates were pushed out of the way for more important discussions. Like the statistics of the Leaf's players and how they trounced Gaspar's favorite Red Wings. When it came to hockey, they only agreed on their mutual dislike of the Montreal Canadians.

* * * *

Despite her nervousness at leaving the house, Mai was glad her friend forced her to come over, and not only because of the lasagna, which tasted so delicious. Mai ate way more than she normally did and then couldn't do anything but lie on the floor and play with Belle. This is what she wanted in her life. A home, a husband, and a little munchkin like her baby Belle.

"What movie do you want to watch, Mai?"

"Oh, I don't care. I'm busy playing with the smartest baby in the universe."

"It was gas, Mai. She didn't smile because she recognized you. She hardly remembers you because I have to bribe you with lasagna to come over."

Even though Stephanie teased her, Mai picked up an odd tone to her friend's voice. "You don't have to bribe me, Steph. It's not that I don't want to come over. I get distracted and caught up with work. I start designing and I might as well be in another world." Mai carefully scooped Belle up off her blanket and carried her over to the sofa. Settling the baby on her shoulder, Belle instantly did the rubbing her nose on Mai's neck that she loved.

"You are in another world when you work. But, honestly Mai, I'm worried you are spending too much time doing that."

"That's my job, Steph. It's how I pay my bills."

"How are the panic attacks?"

"The same and worse." Mai tried not to think about them too much. Even sitting here, she could feel the icy terror at the fringes of her psyche. Stupid, because other than hiding behind her brothers, she couldn't be anywhere safer than here. "I wish I knew how to make them go away."

"Did you go see the doctor?"

"Yes, and he recommended a few different training CDs and wrote me a prescription. Steph, I can't take them. I tried, I really did, but it felt like I was walking around with a wet towel wrapped around my head. I couldn't concentrate on my work, and I felt all stupid. Thinking felt like it took extra effort."

Mai rubbed Belle's back, earning a very loud belch from the innocent face. The unexpected noise made them both laugh. "She learned that from her father."

"Yeah, whatever. You and I have been friends for too long. I know your abilities when it comes to oral gas."

Steph snorted a laugh and covered her mouth.

"Oh god, Steph, tell me you aren't laughing because I said oral?"

Her friend's eyes crinkled in the corners, and she shook her head but didn't take the hand away from her mouth.

"Did someone say 'oral'?" Brodie commented as he walked into the room.

Steph snorted again behind her hand.

"You two were made for each other." Mai looked from Brodie to Steph, who now grinned sappily as soon as her husband spoke.

"You're right. No one could fill my heart like Stephanie." Brodie bent and brushed a quick kiss against his wife's lips before straightening.

"Is she asleep?"

"Almost." Mai shifted Belle from her shoulder. "Goodnight, Princess Bellarina" She pressed a kiss to the baby's warm cheek before she passed her to her father. Brodie scooped her up and settled her into a one handed up in a one-handed football hold, proof that he was very familiar with taking care of his daughter.

"Kiss Mommy good night, Belle of the ball." He held their daughter out, and Stephanie brushed a kiss on her forehead. "Goodnight, baby girl."

Brodie left the room, and Mai found herself staring after him. "Stephanie, you are so lucky." Mai knew that the man of her dreams wasn't going to knock on her apartment door and invite her out for coffee. Since she didn't go out much, she might never find him.

"Yea, I am. And I want you to find your perfect mate as well."

"Mate?"

Stephanie's cheek flushed. "I think I've been reading too many paranormal romance novels. I meant hunny bunny of course."

Mai made a gagging noise and rolled her eyes. "Ew, any man who calls me by anything other than my name will be kicked to the curb."

"You will not because you'll be so much in love you won't care."

"That would be nice. I can't see it happening anytime soon. The thought of going out on a date makes me a nervous wreck." She took a sip of the pop she left on the side table earlier. "I might survive being asked out, but by the time my date arrived, I'd be so worked up I'd probably throw up on his shoes."

"You need to go out on a spontaneous date." Steph nodded her head as if that was the most logical idea ever. "You know if someone asked you out and you went at that moment and didn't have time to get worked up over it."

"Steph, it's not that easy for me. I wish, but I'd launch into a panic attack within moments. I'd make a fool of myself and end up sneaking out of there."

"Okay, then where would you feel safe?"

"My place, but I'm not about to invite some stranger into my home. Let's face it. Until I figure out how to beat this, I'm not going to be doing any dating."

"Don't give up yet, Mai." Steph reached out and patted her hand. "We'll figure out something. You feel safe here, right?"

"Of course."

"Okay then, I'll throw a party and get Brodie to invite a bunch of single guys."

"As long as I'm not the only single woman. I don't want it to be too embarrassing or obvious."

"Nope, I'll talk him into having some guys over to watch a game. Then you can come over and keep me company. Easy peasy."

"I'm lucky to have you as a friend." Mai knew that Steph had her best interests in heart, but eventually she would have to see this mystery guy away from her safety net. Her heart pounded at the thought.

"Yes you are. So, what girly movie are we going to watch tonight? I picked up some extra creamy ice cream from the store.

"Steph, I'm already stuffed."

"A bowl of ice cream won't hurt you. You look like you are losing weight again."

"God, don't tell my mother, she'll freak." Mai knew that she had a habit of skipping meals when she got into her work. Thankfully, Steph kept her eye on her ever since the day Mai admitted that she skipped most meals, hoping that the nauseous feeling that accompanied her panic attacks would stop if she didn't have any food in her stomach. It didn't work. Neither did the lactose products, or any other herbal remedy she tried.

While Steph went to get them some dessert, Mai put in *While You Were Sleeping*. It was a mutual favorite of theirs, and Mai could relate to Sandra Bullock's character. She flopped out on the couch and pressed her feet against the edge of the coffee table.

"I made a special treat for us. Brodie picked up some strawberries from the market this morning." Her best friend grinned and presented her a bowl. "Berries on real vanilla ice cream with chocolate sauce. Perfect for us."

"Looks awesome. Thanks."

"Back in a sec. I'm going to run a bowl up to Brodie."

"Is he not going to join us?"

"No, he says chick flicks give him hives. He's playing *Halo* with his online buddies."

Mai ate some of her ice cream as she waited and tried not to think about how she was going to get her next job. Her life felt like she didn't have any control over it at all lately. Steph sat next to her and put her feet on the coffee table as well. "Okay, now spill. What is bothering you so much tonight?"

Mai told Steph about losing her client and how the thought of trying to find a new one scared her. "I'm so tired of feeling like this." She pressed a chunk of strawberry through the chocolate sauce on her ice cream. "Sometimes, I feel like it will never go away, and I'm going to end up a grumpy old lady, all alone, in a dingy apartment surrounded by a hundred cats."

"No, you won't. I promise we will figure something out. Why don't you stay here tonight?"

"I didn't bring anything with me."

"So, I have lots of clothes that after Belle I don't fit into anymore. You can help yourself to all of them. In the morning, we'll figure out something."

Chapter Two

The next morning, Steph told her about an article she read about people who beat their fears by facing them head-on. They decided that Mai should start by walking downtown during rush hour. If she could manage that, she could move on. Steph drove her close to the downtown core, and Mai hopped out with a promise to call if she needed help.

Typical of the roadwork construction in summer, part of Young Street was pushed into two lanes, which caused all sorts of traffic backups. The smell of asphalt and tar stained the air and soured the pedestrians rushing along the busiest stretch of sidewalk. She did well for a little while until she decided to stretch the day's experiment and take the subway. No sooner had she paid her three fifty and descend the two escalators into the underground did she feel her throat start to close. Determined not to let it win, she continued onto the nearest train.

The crowd closed in around her, and Mai felt her hands begin to shake. *There's no air down here. I'm going to be sick. Everyone will stare...point...laugh...*She could visualize the exact event, and with each passing moment, her heart rate picked up. *I can't breathe.* Her vision wavered, and Mai panicked. The doors shut and so did her chance at escape. *I'm never going to get out of here. Let me out, let me out.*

She gripped the railing and stared out the window at the darkness and flashing lights. Not long, not long, the railcar arrived at the Queen Street station, and Mai stood, surrounded by people. Her throat felt tight, her mouth dry. She couldn't swallow if she wanted to. Finally, after an eternity, the doors opened and she pushed through the crowd, ignoring the noise around her. She didn't see any faces clearly, but everyone looked at her as she tried to escape. Another subway arrived on the other side with a roar, the wind blowing Mai's hair into her face. She fought the crowd as they moved, like a salmon going upstream, only to be swallowed up by the scores of people coming off that train. Pulling her sunglasses down, she covered her eyes and kept her head down. *One foot in front of the other. You can do it, almost there.*

Finally, she raced up the stairwell that burst out onto the street. Thankfully, the sidewalk opened up into a grand entrance of one of the skyscrapers that lined Young Street. Reaching the nearest bench, she flopped down on it and tried not to burst into tears. Taking deep shaking breaths, she tried to get her heart rate down to something other than heart attack speed.

"Are you fucking kidding me? I told you when I placed the order that the goddamn windows had better be ready by today. I have guys at the site waiting to work and nothing there for them to do."

Mai glanced up but didn't see the owner of the voice that echoed around her. It took a moment to locate him, but when she did, her heart skipped a racing beat. A large man stalked across the courtyard toward the hotdog cart set up a few feet away.

"No, we had an agreement asshole, and you are dropping the ball. Get those fucking windows to the site today or I swear this is the last order you will ever see from me."

Okay so the guy could swear like…well, a construction worker. He didn't look like one, dressed in a suit and tie that looked really expensive. One hand held his cell phone against one ear, the other waved as he spoke. Broad-shouldered, he stood about the same height as her brothers, which put him somewhere over six feet. Dark brown hair that hung in waves to just below chin was tucked neatly behind one ear. Sunglasses hid his eyes, but she imagined they would be brown or maybe green. *Oh yeah, someone that sexy looking needs green eyes.*

The lingering edgy feeling Mai felt faded away as she watched the man. Afraid he would notice her looking, she pulled out her phone and pretended to be texting. All the while, she watched him from behind the safety of her dark glasses. He swore a couple more times to the guy on the phone, but the heat seemed to be gone for the moment. He sounded like a complete jerk on the phone at first, but then the conversation shifted to sports and then of course the Leafs. Did anyone in this city talk about anything but hockey? The rush of traffic in front of her and the crowds of people who created noise that echoed off the buildings faded away. For the first moment in what seemed like forever, she felt calmer, as if the panic that usually clawed at her throat retracted its nails allowing her to breath.

"Hey, Chris, let me call you back. I've got to talk to someone more important than you." His laugh echoed around her, a rich sound that made her want to smile in return. How stupid would she look if he caught her staring, but Mai couldn't drag her attention away from him for the world?

"Yeah, fuck you, too. Talk to you later, man."

He passed her and a wind kicked up by a passing truck blew as he pasted in front of her. An incredible smell of wood smoke and spice enveloped her. *Was that his cologne? Damn, he smells good.* He headed straight for the hotdog vendor and ordered a couple sausages.

Mai thought he might be the most gorgeous man she ever saw, and aside from sounding like an asshole at first, he appeared to be a nice guy. Mai had an insane urge to go up and order a hot dog as well. Not that she would actually talk to him, but maybe he would sweep her off her feet and make the world a better place. At least she could stand near him and hope to get a hint of that incredible cologne. *Okay, that sounded weird even to me.*

Caught in her imagination for a minute, she enjoyed watching him and the vendor chat about something as he polished off a sausage. She couldn't understand a word they were saying. It sounded European. In a city like Toronto one got used to the continuous wave of various languages spoken. Lost in her own thoughts, she almost missed the guy leaving. Sadly, he headed into the lobby of the building in front of her, one of the many financial towers around. As he left, the world came back into focus again. The constant honk and rush of traffic, the ding of the buses and streetcars as they passed intruded into her peaceful little world.

Feeling much calmer than she had in the longest time, Mai took a deep breath of city air. Better to get back out of here and into the suburbs again where the air felt a bit cleaner and not so smoggy. Even though the weatherman had forecasted it to be mild, downtown always felt hotter and more humid.

She got to her feet and walked toward the vendor, not certain why, but part of her wasn't willing to let her imaginary guy go yet. Why didn't she get up and do something while he stood here? *Because you're a chicken and he is way out of your league.* At times, she really did hate that inner voice of hers. Confident men like that wanted women the same way. She couldn't be that person. Especially not now when her experiment on the subway failed so spectacularly. No point in being any more depressed then she already felt.

"Can I help you?" The vendor stared at her waiting for her order.

Can you tell me anything about the gorgeous man you were speaking to? "I'd like water please."

* * * *

Vencel paused before he pushed the elevator button. Something tugged at his subconscious as if he dropped something or forgot it. He still held on to his BlackBerry, his sunglasses were on his head, and his wallet in his back pocket. He glanced over at the clear glass walls of the lobby. No one looked at him or watched him. *What the hell?* He couldn't shake the feeling that he missed something important.

A *ding* sounded in front of him, and the stainless steel elevator doors opened. A perfectly coiffed, gorgeous blonde woman stood there. Her clothes closely followed her curves, and her skirt was short enough to display a pair of shapely, long legs, and a pair of wicked looking black heels. She didn't hesitate to check him out from head to toe as he stepped inside. Bold, assertive, and not afraid to go after what she wanted. He knew this type, a gold digger who no doubt had a sugar daddy somewhere in the building but was always looking to trade up to a better deal.

Nodding slightly, he pressed the button for the eleventh floor and stepped away from her and pretended to be texting on his BlackBerry to avoid having to talk to her. Thankfully, she got off at the next floor, and he glanced up in time to see her wink at him. That kind of woman was more of a predator than him. Her claws would tear his heart out so she could press her stiletto heel into the middle. He looked back down and ignored her. Women like that always took care of themselves. He learned that lesson a long time ago and wasn't about to get trapped again. The doors slid shut, and he breathed a sigh of relief as the car continued on its upward journey.

Last night's conversation with Gaspar echoed in his memories. His brother, the eternal optimist, seemed so convinced that their mate hid around the next corner. Vencel would love to find the perfect woman to share with his brother, but did she really exist? Could there be a woman out there strong enough to withstand all the secrets? They had met many female werewolves since moving here, but not a one appealed to both him and his brother and, more importantly, to their wolves.

A soft *ping* heralded his arrival, and the doors opened again. He stepped out into the reception area of a firm that researched federal logging practices. They were the ones who watched the logging companies to make certain they followed the rules. Their recent focus was on the practices used in Algonquin Forest. Ironically, werewolves ran almost the entire firm, fitting in Vencel's book since they had a vested interest in preserving the forests. Algonquin Park stretched almost nine thousand square miles, approximately the same size as the state of New Jersey. In wolf form, Gordon's people watched and noted any infractions, and he stepped in and immediately corrected the situation.

"Hello, Mr. Sofalvi."

Vencel smiled at the woman sitting behind the large desk. She didn't bother to look up, but he could feel her displeasure when he perched a hip against her domain. "Jessica, how many times have I asked you to call me by my first name?"

"Almost every time you have been here I would imagine." She continued to type away at her keyboard, keeping her back to him. Jessica was stubborn, strong-willed, and tough. She controlled everyone who came through those doors and made certain that her Alpha always had what he needed, usually before he knew he needed it. She was everything he thought he wanted in a woman, but his wolf disagreed. The wolf wanted a woman who needed them. Vencel wanted a woman who could take care of herself. Weak women got themselves killed, and he wasn't willing to lose another one.

"If you would *take a seat* in one of the chairs and not on my desk, I'm certain I can get you into the office sooner than later." She kept her back to him and continued to type.

"No, I think I'd like to visit with you instead." He picked up her stapler and looked at it before putting it back down in a different spot. "How is your family? I heard that your brother had been promoted to Guardian in the pack."

The position of Guardian in the pack was much like a human soldier. They acted under the Alpha's direct orders to keep the pack safe and protected. They also policed their own kind and enforced the pack rules when necessary.

Jessica reached out and moved her stapler back into its proper spot, and then resumed typing. Vencel poked at a pad of paper and moved it a few inches over, smiling when she stopped typing and huffed out a breath.

"Daniel is very happy with his new position, not that it was a big surprise. We all knew he was born to that position." She reached over and moved her yellow pad back into its place.

"He's not the only one. I know you have a protective streak a mile wide." Her shoulders stiffened slightly, not that he would have noticed if he hadn't been watching. Jessica looked as if she would snap if she tried to bend. He reached for the picture frame and looked at the photo within. It must have been taken recently, but she looked like a different person in it. Her hair curled wildly around her face, unlike the normal slick, tight twist she wore it in, and she was laughing in the arms of her brother who looked to be in the process of tickling her. "I never would have thought you to be ticklish."

Jessica spun abruptly in her chair. Reaching out, she plucked the frame from his fingers. "Mr. Roberts will see you now, Vencel."

"Now was that so difficult?" He leaned over and pressed a quick kiss against her forehead, a casual sign among them that he was happy with her decision. She didn't say anything but turned back to her computer screen and began typing again. Despite her abrupt movements, Vencel could see a slight softening of her posture. He pushed himself back to his feet and knocked on the heavy wooden door before opening it.

Gordon didn't speak until the door closed behind him. "Are you picking on my assistant again, Vencel?"

"Yes."

Gordon met Vencel in the middle of the room, and they shook hands. Vencel lowered his gaze in respect to the Alpha before looking back up at him. "Good. She needs to be picked on a bit. Something is up with that girl, and she's going to snap from the stress soon."

"I got the impression that something was going on with her. Can't you make her tell you?"

"Yes, I could, but I don't rule like that. My wolves have their own lives, and I don't interfere unless it threatens the pack." He moved behind his desk and sat down, relaxing back against the leather seat. "But if she doesn't talk soon, I'm going to step in."

"Is that why I'm here?" This meeting was at Gordon's request, and Vencel wasn't completely certain why.

"Yes and no. I've been hearing a lot of talk about the Hungarian wolves. Specifically your old pack. Were you and your brother thinking of returning to your home country?"

"Canada is our home." Vencel sat down in a chair on the other side of Gordon's desk. "Shouldn't Gaspar be here for this conversation?"

"I expect he will be arriving any moment. I asked him to come in shortly after you did."

As if speaking his name conjured him, the door opened and Gaspar waltzed in. "Until later, Jessica, my sweet." He called out over his shoulder.

"You're a menace." While her words sounded angry, Vencel could hear the humor behind them.

Gaspar patted Vencel's shoulder in greeting before shaking Gordon's hand over his desk. He, too, lowered his eyes in respect to the older man. Neither he nor Gaspar wanted control over the pack, so they were careful to never give Gordon a reason to feel as if he was being challenged.

"What did you find out?" Gordon asked his brother.

"I think she is having financial difficulties. Didn't you say she had hooked up with a human boyfriend? I think the guy is controlling her more than she wants to admit. She isn't wearing much in the way of makeup, and I've never seen her pull her hair back so severely."

"You don't like to interfere?" Vencel grinned as he spoke the words to Gordon, who arched an eyebrow.

"I will do anything for my wolves even if he means using your brother's gift for getting woman to talk."

Gaspar shrugged "I do what little I can, but in all seriousness, I would keep a close eye on him. I don't think she's being abused, but it might be a matter of time. Want me to pay him a visit?"

Gaspar had a soft spot for women he thought needed protecting, and if he got involved, this human could end up with a wolf bite on his ass.

"No, I don't want her to know yet. Hopefully, she will get herself out of this. That isn't everything I wanted to talk to you both about. As I was telling your brother, I have been hearing rumors about your old pack."

"What kind of rumors?"

"They want their princes back."

That bit of truth hung in the air around them. Gordon never asked them about their past, respecting their need for privacy. But this kind of information he would have to act on.

"Gordon, neither Vencel nor myself have any interest in ruling a pack, Hungarian or Canadian. We've spoken about going back, but only for a visit to old friends."

"If that is the case, then the time has come for the two of you to take a solid position within the pack."

"What do you mean?"

"I mean that both of you have lived on the fringes of our society, and I can accept your need for privacy. However, I would like the two of you to consider taking positions of liaisons within the pack. Given the obvious strength you both have, it would help the weaker wolves to understand your position, and both of you are strong enough to take over if something happened to me."

"Is there something else you want to tell us?"

Gordon wasn't an old man by any means. Vencel suspected that he might have passed his first century, but that was it. The silver that streaked through the man's black hair was because of the close relationship he had with his wolf and not due to age.

"No. But, if we are going to have the older packs sniffing around my territory, then I don't want to be caught with my pants down. Algonquin is a massive area, and there are other shape-shifters moving into the fringes of my territory. It's big enough for us all, but I need someone to keep an eye on them. There are a few established packs living peacefully within the Adirondack Park, and I would prefer Algonquin follow their lead.

"Has anyone approached you yet?" Vencel knew they were being given this position because a civil war and territorial disputes drove them from Hungary during the war. Neither he nor Gaspar wanted to ever see the same thing happen here.

"I don't want an answer right now, but I'd like the two of you to think about it."

Chapter Three

"Miss Bennett? Mai Bennett?"

Mai looked up from her BlackBerry at the man standing in front in her. Amazement robbed her of a voice. He was tall, very broad, with large, muscular arms that almost stretched the sleeves of his T-shirt, and she would bet her life savings that he sported a full six-pack of abs. He didn't look like one of those pretty boys that shopped on Young Street. He looked like a man used to working for a living. Dark hair framed his face. All one length, it curled below his chin and looked as if he ran his fingers through it a lot. His skin looked well-tanned, and the lighter sun-bleached streaks in his hair along with his well-tanned skin made her think he must work outside a lot. *Why the hell is he talking to me?*

He pushed his sunglasses up to the top of his head, catching his hair in the process and pulling it back from his face. It struck her then why he looked familiar. This was the same guy she saw at the hot dog stand outside the Star building a few days ago. She wondered then what his eyes looked like, and now she knew. His eyes were an incredible amber color that made her want to stare into them all day.

"You are Mai Bennett?"

"Oh, yes. Sorry, I was in my own world there for a moment." She could feel a wave of heat burn her skin. She hoped it looked like too much sun. "Do I know you?"

Amusement shone on his face, and she figured that he knew why she hadn't spoken right away. Strike one for arrogance, even if she had acted all moony a moment ago.

"No, you don't, but I'm hoping to change that." He waved to the seat next to her. "My name is Gaspar Sofalvi. May I sit down?"

"I'm waiting for a friend." Mai looked around expecting to see Stephanie bounce around the corner with baby Belle strapped to her in the baby sling. "She's late."

He sat down on the bench next to her and stretched an arm along the back. "Your friend, Stephanie? She didn't tell you, did she?"

"Tell me what?"

"You're meeting me, not her."

Mai blinked. *Oh no she wouldn't...actually, yes she would.* "You're telling me my soon-to-be ex-best friend set me up on a blind date and didn't tell me?"

"Don't drop her as a friend yet, and yes, that is exactly what she did. I think she was worried that if she told you beforehand, you wouldn't come."

I'm going to kill her. Of course Mai wouldn't have shown up. Being stuck with someone she didn't know guaranteed her to get hit with a couple of panic attacks. It was then she realized the normal icy feelings weren't freezing her chest. She felt safe and protected. She couldn't remember the last time she felt so alive. Why now?

"Why would you need to be set up on a blind date?" Mai didn't want to sound rude, but she was practical. Men like him didn't give her the time of day because they were way out of her league.

"I'm friends with her husband."

"Brodie, really?"

"He's talked about you a few times, and I wanted to meet you. He really likes you."

"I like him, too, and not just because he lets Stephanie get away with everything and then helps her fix it whenever her crazy ideas go wrong."

"But I'm not here to talk about them. I want to get to know you." He stroked her hair with his fingertips, a smile playing at his lips. *It shouldn't be legal for a man to have such incredible lips.*

"Come on." He grabbed her hand and gave it a light tug. "Let's go for a walk."

She expected him to let go as soon as she stood, but instead he held on for a moment and ran his thumb along the back of her hand. "Your skin is very soft." He didn't step back when she stood, so she ended up very close to him. Again she expected the normal wave of nervousness to overwhelm her, but those negative feelings didn't have a chance against Gaspar's presence.

She looked up at his face and felt the intensity burning in his gaze. She didn't completely understand why he would look at her that way. *Are his lips as soft as they look?* It would be so easy lift up and kiss him. *Would he let me? Would he lean down and meet me halfway?* For an insane moment, she almost followed through. When she shifted her weight to her toes, the small voice in the back of her head screeched a warning. *What are you doing!* Mai stepped quickly away, horrified by what she almost did. Of all the socially inept things to try. *Holy crap, he's a stranger, and I almost threw myself at his head.*

"I don't think this is a good idea." She heard herself say the words, but she wouldn't look at him. She didn't want to see the disgust on his face.

"Hey, don't toss our date aside already. Please, Mai, give me a chance?"

Mai darted a quick look at him, thankful for her own sunglasses. Hopefully they would block him from seeing what crazy impulses bombarded her inside. Maybe all that happened in her head, and he didn't notice a thing?

"Mai is an interesting name. I don't mean any offense, but you don't look Asian."

Mai smiled, the assumption of Asian heritage was a common mistake many people made before they met her. "It means Cherry Blossom. My parents loved to travel, and according to Mom, I was conceived in Vietnam. Also, she craved those chocolate-covered cherries for her entire pregnancy."

"Do you have any siblings?"

"Yes, two older brothers who both think they were put on this earth to tease me."

Gaspar laughed. "I bet they are very protective of you."

"Yes, that, too." Mai felt herself relax a bit more as the two of them walked down one of the many paths.

"Were your parents traveling during their conception as well?"

This time Mai laughed. "Yes. Jelani, my oldest brother, was conceived in Africa and Marcario in South America. They both travel a lot as well. Jelani is a nurse with Doctors Without Borders, and Marcario is an architect who helps to build schools in needy countries."

"They sound like very good men."

"They are, and I'm really proud of them. I don't do anything as important as them. I'm just a computer geek."

"Considering how much our world relies on computers, I would say that your chosen career is very important as well."

"Nah, we're a dime a dozen now a days." Mai waved her hand a bit. "What about you? Gaspar is an interesting name."

He tucked Mai's hand into his arm. An old-fashioned move she saw in a movie once, but she liked the feeling of his bicep under her hand.

"It's Hungarian, and since that is where I was born, I think it's safe to say my parents followed your parents' trend to choose their children names from where they were conceived. I have a younger brother, Vencel, who I think is much too serious, and I do my best to pester him as much as possible."

"I think our families are very similar then. When did you come to Canada?"

"Vencel and I emigrated here after our parents passed away."

"Oh, I'm so sorry." Mai felt her throat tighten in sympathy.

"I didn't want to make you sad, Mai. It happened a long time ago. What about your parents?"

"Brodie didn't tell you?"

Gaspar shook his head.

"My dad passed from cancer when I seventeen. My mom never fully recovered from it I'm afraid. She's a wonderful person but a bit hollow. She rejoined the Peace Corps a few years ago and tries to help other people."

"What about you, Mai? If your family travels so much, who takes care of you?"

"I take care of myself, of course." Mai tried to keep her voice upbeat, but he wouldn't let her pull her arm away from his when she tried.

"I get the impression you are a very strong person, Mai."

"No, really I'm not." *I feel like I'm going insane to be honest.*

"I can't believe that. In fact, I bet you are brave enough to face some of the wildest animals I have ever met."

They strolled through High Park, stopping at the petting zoo the park sponsored. He paid for some feed, and the two of them faced the ravages of crazed goats and fed them. Mai couldn't remember a time she laughed so much.

That funniest part was the goats kept running away from him and would surround her. She tried to hand him the food, but they scattered no matter what they did. "What's your cologne, Eau de Predator?" Mai teased him as the goats stampeded away from him for the fourth time.

The look of surprise on his face made her laugh even harder. "All right that's enough."

Mai's world literally turned upside down when he bent down and scooped her up over his shoulder as if she didn't weigh a thing.

"Ah!" She laughed and smacked him on the lower back. "Put me down, you Neanderthal." She braced her hands on his back and tried to wriggle free, but he clamped a strong arm around her legs. "You might be able to intimidate the poor, helpless goats, but you don't scare me." That realization stuck in her head for a moment, making her heart skip a beat. *I'm not afraid of him.* She waved to the petting zoo attendant who opened the gate and let them out. The old man shook his head, laughing at their antics.

They spent the next few hours tossing bread to the ducks, talking and pausing to enjoy the park. In that time Mai felt herself become more and more comfortable with Gaspar. When he reached over and took her hand, she didn't pull away from him. They wandered around hand in hand, people watching and talking about the things that interested them. She learned quickly that Gaspar loved any kind of sports, but he and his brother were especially passionate about hockey. His voice carried a soft hint of an accent that she loved the sound of and could have listened to all day. Unfortunately, he insisted she tell him about herself.

She told him about her plans to grow her website designs and about what life was like when she went to high school. She and her brothers were home schooled, because her parents still loved to travel to different countries to help out where they could. Once she and her brothers reached high school, her parents moved back to Canada so they could attend school. The boys quickly became popular because of their looks and easy-going attitudes. Being insanely good at sports helped, too. They were in grades eleven and twelve when Mai started grade nine. Mai stuck to the shadows and avoided the spotlight as best she could. Sure there were girls that wanted to be her friend but only because they had a crush on one of her brothers.

"How did you meet Stephanie?"

"Steph was the first person to ever stick up for me. Don't get me wrong, my brothers didn't pick on me. But, they were teenage boys, and I'm certain you can imagine what their priorities were at that age."

"Oh, I think I can guess. A little sister didn't hold a high enough position on their priority list."

"No, especially since I've always been completely useless in sports and spent most of my time reading or playing video games."

"One day, an especially pushy girl was giving me a hard time, and Steph came out of nowhere. She isn't the tallest person, but when her temper is up, she gets this presence about her. She might as well been six feet tall the way she stomped in and started giving this chick shit for picking on me. We've been friends ever since."

"Her family is my family, and Brodie is like another brother to me now."

She glanced around and noticed that they had wandered into a slightly secluded area. "Where are we going?"

Gaspar stepped behind a large oak tree and trapped her between it and his large form. "For the record, Mai, I'm not interested in you thinking of me as a brother." He bent his head and kissed her on the cheek, then moved closer and brushed his lips against hers.

Anticipation blossomed in her chest, relighting all her nerve endings. It had been so very long since someone kissed her like this. "I don't think I'll ever look at you as a brother."

He rested his arm against the tree bark above her head and leaned over her. His hand wrapped around her neck where it met her shoulder. His thumb pressed gently against the underside of her chin. "I don't want to be your friend either."

Mai could feel her pussy getting wet, and right now she wanted more than anything to do something wild and crazy. "How can you be certain you don't want to be friends?"

He smiled down at her, and his hand slid down, his fingers tracing her collarbone. "Because friends don't have sex because they are afraid to ruin things. I very much want to have sex with you."

"Oh." Mai blinked up at him, robbed of speech. It wasn't that his blunt words were a turn off. The opposite was true. She couldn't believe that someone would want to do that with her.

"The minute I saw you, I knew you were special."

This could all be an elaborate scheme to get into her pants, but Mai didn't care. She lived life so very carefully and look where it got her. This one time she wanted to do something completely out of character and spontaneous. She wanted to be one of the bad girls, and if it meant that Gaspar never called her again, then at least she had this one time.

His hand slid over her collarbone and down until he cupped one of her breasts. Her nipple pebbled under his palm, and she instinctively arched into his caress. The afternoon was warm, but here in the trees the temperature felt a bit cooler, especially against her hot skin. "I want to lay you out in the sun and lick every inch of your skin from the toes up."

"I think I could handle that."

"Good. We'll make it our second date." He slid his hand under her T-shirt and stroked the warm skin of her stomach before sliding a hand up between her breasts. A simple pinch on the closure of her bra and it snapped open. "Mai, lift your shirt for me."

"Oh um…" Mai let go of one of his shoulders and gripped the bottom of her shirt. She paused for a moment, feeling a bit self-conscious.

"Come on, Mai. I can't hold onto your shirt and worship your skin at the same time. I need your help."

She slowly lifted her small T-shirt until both her breasts peaked out from underneath. "You are so incredibly beautiful." Gaspar cupped his hands around her breasts and flicked her nipples with his tongue. It felt like there was a nerve cluster that ran directly to her throbbing clit. Now that is why she would love for him to wrap his lips around her there. He sucked her breasts deep into his mouth, and then bit down gently. She jumped at the electrical current that seemed to run through her body, only to feel her legs begin to shake and her core throb with need.

Gaspar paid equal attention to each of her breasts, laving them with attention while keeping them cupped in his large hands

"Are we really going to do this?" Mai felt as though her skin was on fire and Gaspar the only way to soothe it. He cupped her face in his hands, and she looked up into those incredible eyes.

"God, I hope so, Mai. I can't explain right now why, but I want to be inside you more than anything." Mai couldn't explain this wild need that gripped her either, but she wanted more than anything for him to do exactly what he said. His lips met hers as his tongue swept into her mouth. He tasted like chocolate popsicles and pure decadence. When he lifted his mouth from hers, Mai speared her fingers through his hair and tried to stop him. "I'll stop if you say so, Mai. I swear, I don't want you to do anything you don't want to do.

"Don't you dare stop anything." Mai felt wild and free. Pressed up against a tree with an incredibly handy man between her legs made her feel freer than she ever had before.

"I don't want anyone to see you like this."

"Then stop wasting time."

He grinned, and she felt him lower her to her feet and reached for the buttons on her shorts as she grabbed for the same on his jeans. Her hands shook with need but Gaspar won the race. He slowly lowered her shorts over her hips, pressing a kiss to her lower tummy and then to the small patch of curls between her legs. She felt his tongue dart out, spearing between her folds and licking her clit. She cried out, and Gaspar stood up immediately. "Shhhhh, Mai. You don't want to draw a crowd, do you?"

At this point she didn't care. All she wanted to feel him inside of her. She felt a wrapped condom being placed in her hand. "Here, put this on me."

This taste of reality allowed her to come back to her own for a second. She darted a look around, but they still remained secluded behind the thick patch of trees. She tore open the package and took out the condom. She slid her hand over Gaspar's large cock. It stood out from his body, dark red and hot to the touch. Running her fingers over its length made Gaspar suck in a deep breath between his teeth. "Don't tease, please."

His voice sounded lower than it had been, and his eyes almost looked lighter. It had to be a trick from the dappled light around them.

She rolled the sheath down his length, and as soon as she finished Gaspar grasped her around her chest and lifted her up against the tree. Mai wrapped her legs around his hips, and her hands gripped his shoulders.

He stepped closer, and she had a moment of concern he might not fit when the blunt head of his cock pressed against her weeping opening. Her body stretched in acceptance as he pushed inside her. The long unused muscles of her body stretched to the point of burning, but Mai needed more. Gaspar pulled back and then slid deeper. Each stroke robbed her of her breath. The next left her gasping.

Her nerves snapped like a broken electrical wire, and she tried to keep her mouth closed and not scream out like she so desperately wanted to. Gaspar's fingers gripped her hips tightly. She would have bruises left, but she really didn't care. In fact, she hoped she did as proof that this was real. "Oh god, Mai. You're so fucking tight. You're perfect."

He whispered a bit more in a language she didn't understand, but even if he had spoken English, she wasn't certain that she would have understood it. The feelings inside her pounded against her skin to the pulse his rhythm dictated. He kissed her with an intensity she didn't know could be possible. His tongue stroked her mouth to the same beat, as he slipped his fingers between their bodies and pinched her hard little clit. Mai screamed into his mouth, digging her heels into his lower back. She could feel her body clenching his, milking him. He pulled almost all the way out and then swiftly pushed back inside in one long stroke. Gripping her hips, he did it again and again. Each stroke extended the incredible sensations pulsing through her. He picked up speed, and she wrapped her arms around him, clawing at his back. Concentrating, she squeezed her muscles as he pulled out. Gaspar grunted and bit the side of her neck, sending a shock wave straight to her core. She did it again, and this time he dropped his head against her shoulder and shook, pulling her body down against him. A low growl vibrated against her skin and she felt him throb deep within her. The intensity of the moment pulled another shuddering orgasm from her.

They both stood there panting for air, and Mai felt like her legs were made of taffy. There was no way she could stand on them. Gaspar withdrew from inside her, leaving her feeling incredibly empty. He kissed her forehead and then the corner of her mouth. "Are you okay?"

Mai opened her eyes and smiled at him. At the height he held her, his eyes were level with hers. She looked deep into his amber eyes and wondered if it might be possible to fall in love in an afternoon.

"You're an incredible woman, Mai. Now that I've met you, I don't ever want to lose you."

"You felt it, too, right? We're not moving too fast are we?"

"We were meant to be together." He caressed her cheek with the back of his hand. "I want to take you out to the best dinner you have ever had tonight."

"Really, you don't have to." He lowered her to the ground. She leaned back against the tree when her feet touched the ground. Her soul still felt like it was floating.

"I want to." He bent down and picked up her shorts. Placing one of her hands on his shoulder, he held them open. She stepped into them, and he pulled them up and did the button.

"Um, Gaspar. You forgot my underwear."

"No I didn't." He slipped her flip-flops back on her feet before standing back up. He kissed her and wrapped his hands over her bottom, sliding over the globes of her ass. "I want to continue our walk and know that you aren't wearing anything under those shorts." Then he broke away from the kiss and scooped her underwear off the ground and pushed them in his pocket. "As for dinner, you pick the place and that's where we will go."

"Taste of the Danforth is on tonight, but I don't know if we can get tickets at this late time." The annual event featured all the best restaurants on the Danforth. They prepared their best dishes, and each restaurant had limited seating.

"Don't you worry about that. I'll take care of it."

Chapter Four

"Vencel, dammit, you have a phone. Why don't you answer it!" Gaspar paced the length of his condo. He couldn't wait for his brother to meet Mai, and not because he had a burning urge to say I told you so, although he might work it into conversation at some point.

His heart hadn't stopped racing from the moment he strolled up the path at the park. Her scent floated on the warm breeze, and it almost brought him to his knees. She smelled like the sweetest flowers, like a forest after a spring rain. She smelled like home. It amazed him how life worked sometimes because as soon as her scent hit his nose, it filled a void in his soul that he didn't realize existed until now.

Finally, after what seemed like a hundred rings, Vencel's voice mail kicked in.

"I found her, our mate. She is the most incredible woman you will ever meet. I'm taking her out to dinner tonight. I want you to come and meet her. You can pretend you're me at first. Get to know her when she is relaxed. She is a nervous person, and I don't want to overwhelm her. We'll come clear shortly after. Vencel she tastes so good, wait till you taste her pussy. I got a brief taste today, and I've been craving more ever since I took her home. You know that might have been the dumbest thing I've ever done. I should have brought her home."

He didn't have the words to describe how he felt buried deep inside her, feeling her heels digging into his lower back as he rocked against her soft body. He could close his eyes and almost imagine her scent and taste it on his tongue. Tonight he planned to lay her back and spread those long legs of hers and dine till she came all over his tongue. He had to remember how delicate she was. When he helped her into her shorts, he saw the marks he left on her hips today. Part of that horrified him, but the animal inside him liked that he marked her. Physically, she might be delicate, but she had a heart of gold. Also she carried an inner strength that he didn't think she knew she had.

One thing he would insist on of his mate was no more tearing herself down. It really angered him when she didn't give herself the credit she earned. Many times he heard her hide behind her fears or brush off an accomplishment. He could sense a deep fear that had a hold of her soul. Every time it rose close to the surface, Gaspar could feel the hair on the back of his neck stand up.

"I'm taking her to the Taste the Danforth event tonight, eight thirty seating." He wanted Mai to do some exploring of different foods tonight. He didn't ask her why she didn't travel as well. It must be in her blood since every other family member of hers tended to have a nomadic tendency. Not Mai, she sat in her apartment on her computer. "You and I can trade places at one of the restaurants. You better call me back and soon. Trust me, she's the one." He hung up without telling his brother anything else and finished getting ready. That message should catch Vencel's attention.

Vencel had to meet her. There would be no convincing him otherwise that she was their mate. His brother tended to be a pessimist about most things, but then the wars affected them in different ways.

He wanted to pick Mai up at her apartment, but she insisted on meeting him down at Union Station, and for now he would let her keep him at a distance. Mai might tell him a lot about her family and friends, but she didn't reveal much about herself. He might have gotten her to open up to him, but he knew she hid behind her walls. That is the Mai he wanted to know. He could sense the strength deep within her even if she didn't.

More importantly, his animal recognized its mate. Mating a human wasn't all that common to their people, but was frowned upon in Hungary. Here in Canada, he met a number of shape-shifters who found their true mate in a human. After the bonding, the humans lived as long as their mate.

He couldn't wait for Mai and Vencel to meet. Part of him didn't like the idea of deceiving her, but he didn't want to frighten her off already. Let her get used to him and then Vencel, and once he felt convinced she wasn't going to run on him, he would tell her the rest.

* * * *

The gods were bitter nasty creatures that obviously favored their precious humans. Why else would a race of helpless creatures rule the earth and hunt those that were stronger?

He sent a quick text to his brother.

Here

Gaspar's reply was almost immediate.

I'll be out front in a moment

As Vencel waited, he watched a couple of over-processed women teeter on incredibly high heels as they tried to leave the restaurant and call a cab. *Oh please don't let one of them be her.*

A waft of perfume hit his olfactory senses like a sledgehammer. Had they never heard of less is more? Turning his head, he sneezed into his sleeve and blinked. His nose felt like it had yards of cotton batting packed into it. He needed to get out of the city for a week or two. This smog was killing him, or at least it felt like it.

He walked up the steps and entered the restaurant. The hostess blinked at him in surprise. He smiled at her the same way Gaspar would and walked into the restaurant as if he had only stepped out for a moment. He followed the directions that Gaspar texted him to let him know which table he and this woman were sitting at. Let Gaspar figure out an excuse for why he was in two different places. The woman sat with her back in his direction, allowing him to quickly sit.

She jumped slightly and looked behind her in surprise. "Sorry, I didn't expect you to come back that way."

"Is there a rule in here which way a table can be approached?"

"Um no, I guess not." Thankfully she fell silent. Now if he could get through the next little while without having to talk too much, then perhaps he could get out of here quicker. Only dinner Gaspar said. Eat and then pack her into a cab and send her home.

He glanced up at her, surprised at how pretty she was. He expected different. Not entirely certain what he expected, but with a name like Mai, he didn't expect her to be as tall. She needed to put on some weight, and the way she appeared to be picking at her salad wouldn't do it. "You should eat more than salad."

"You said that already."

Not surprising since he and Gaspar shared the same taste in women, but it wouldn't look good to blow this already. He lifted the bottle of champagne from the ice bucket. "Would you like another drink?"

"Oh, no thank you. You go ahead."

Vencel shrugged and knocked back the wine in his glass before topping Gaspar's glass back up. Glancing at the bottle he almost sprayed the wine in his mouth. 1988 Vintage Krug? *Fuck me sideways.* Either Gaspar felt he needed something to salvage his dinner date, or he considered this a celebration. Since he was certain he found their mate, celebrating must be the excuse for blowing almost a grand on a bottle of bubbles.

His phone chirped. *Jesus, Gaspar's such a fuss pot.* He knew how to speak to a woman without prompting. "Oh, sorry about that." He reached into his jacket pocket and turned off the phone without looking at it. Serve his meddling brother right.

"How's your salad?"

"It's fine, thank you." She fidgeted in her seat and glanced around the room. Interesting, each time she did, her eyes focused on the exits. Was Gaspar that distracted with the thought of their mate being close that he almost bombed out his dinner date? He would try his best to salvage what he could. He would never admit it to his brother, but he wasn't as eloquent as Gaspar, and if his brother did a lousy job, then he couldn't be anything but an improvement.

"I really should admit something."

Vencel looked over at the woman across from him. She was so quiet. Time to play the interested dinner date. "What's that?"

"I've seen you before."

"Really? Where's that?"

"Downtown. I saw you at the plaza. You were getting a sausage from the vendor there." She laughed, nervousness making her laugh sounding like shattered glass. "I didn't know you were a friend of Brodie's."

A cold shiver ran down Vencel's spine. Great, another gold digger, as if he didn't have enough of those in his life. He didn't know who this Brodie was, but he wouldn't allow this charade to go on. The last thing he needed was another woman interested in his bank account.

"I don't think I'm who you think I am."

"Yes, I think you are. Or you are his clone."

"I don't go downtown often unless I'm working, and I don't work out of the plaza buildings."

"I don't understand. I thought you said you lived down there."

So she managed to get that information out of Gaspar. He wondered if she also managed to get his annual salary. Damn, his bother needed to learn to be more discreet. "You hired me lady. You know the kind of work I do."

Her fork stopped halfway to her lips, leaving her mouth in an *O* shape. An insane thought slipped through his brain, the idea of slipping his cock into that shape and opening her up even more. She placed the fork on the table and wiped her hands on her napkin. The color drained from her face somewhat making him feel bad. But he didn't know what he did wrong. She hired Gaspar, maybe she didn't want to have it brought up. He knew damn well that Gaspar didn't do surprise jobs. He didn't understand the playing. His brother hadn't said anything about this being a role-playing night.

"What did you say?"

"Sorry. I forgot the boundaries we set for the evening. Forget I mentioned it."

"Are you saying that you were paid to come on a date with me?"

Vencel didn't think her porcelain skin cold get any paler. He was wrong. "Are you all right? Your color isn't good."

"I'm not feeling very well at the moment." She pulled her shawl up over her shoulders with shaking hands. "Please excuse me for a moment. I'll be right back."

She started to get up, but the threads hanging off her flimsy shawl got caught in the swirls in the back of the chair. She plunked back down in her seat and tried to pull them loose, but her hands shook so badly that she only made it worse. He didn't need his nose to be working to know that he had offended her.

"Here, let me help." He reached over, but she pulled away before he ever touched her.

"No." She jerked out of the way and leaped to her feet. A few of the patrons glanced over their way. Mai looked around and noticed something that made her look on the verge of dissolving into tears. Guilt pounded against him. He shouldn't have assumed anything, and now he upset her. Gaspar would kick his ass for putting a nasty blot on his pristine record. "Listen, I apologize. That was rude of me. When you come back, we'll pretend it never happened." He caught her hand and pressed his lips to it. Her skin felt so silky under his fingers, he brushed his lips against her knuckles loving the sensitivity of her delicate skin under his lips. She jerked her hand from his and rubbed at the place he kissed. Her face lacked all color except for a stark splash of red across her cheek.

"Excuse me."

She practically ran from the dining room, her pace was so quick. He leaned to the side and enjoyed the way her skirt swirled around her legs. She had very long legs, and he wondered if the skin on her inner thigh tasted as incredible as the back of her hand. Logically, she would be even silkier there, and that close to her pussy, even with a plugged nose, he would be able to smell her.

He watched as she headed for the back of the restaurant and no doubt to go to the washroom to re-plan her attack. He cut a slice off his brother's steak and popped it into his mouth. Damn the meat was good here, almost as good if he hunted it himself.

* * * *

Deep breath. Deep breath. One foot in front of the other. Mai tried to walk a straight line, despite the way her body shook. Was she staggering? She didn't feel secure. She felt like she had the rug ripped out from under her. And Steph? Why would she do this? Did she want to make a fool of her? Her stomach cramped, and a wave of fear rolled over her. She felt as though she might be sick. Right here, right now, in the middle of an expensive restaurant in front of everyone. *Were they staring at her? Would they point and laugh?* She felt like a piece of glass that cracked in a thousand spider's legs, and one more tiny knock and she would shatter.

One foot in front of the other. She could do it. Just a few seconds more. A few more steps and she could make it out of the restaurant. Passing the washroom doors, she glanced over her shoulder, but Gaspar wasn't following her. She couldn't see him from here.

"Is everything all right?" The hostess stepped in front of Mai, looking more than a bit suspicious.

"I'm fine, but my date went sour. He's still at the table. You might as well get the waitress to bring him the bill. I'm leaving."

"Oh, all right. Would you like me to pass on a message?"

Yes, he is an arrogant, rude Neanderthal who I hope chokes on his steak. "No, I need to leave." Mai could feel her throat closing up. Panic fluttered wildly at her throat, wrapping around it, making her feel like she couldn't breathe.

She pushed past the waitress and rushed out the doors that lead to a patio out back. He might have seen her if she left through the front door. Speed walking along the sidewalk, she swallowed the frantic flutter of her gag reflex. Her body felt like it was made from jelly. Her legs felt rubbery, and all she wanted to do was cry. She scanned the street for a taxi, but the available ones rushed by. She could wave one down, but that would bring attention to herself. She darted a look over her shoulder again. *Was she being followed? What if leaving him there made him mad and he comes after me?* She picked up the pace until she practically ran down the street. Passing the subway, she wished she could run down there and disappear with the crowds.

A ding sounded ahead, and she realized that one of the TTC rockets was heading in her direction. She loved the red rocket streetcars in Toronto. Darting across a pause in traffic, she hopped on board. Digging in her small purse she pulled out enough change to pay and then went and took a seat in the corner next to the doorway. At least from here she could feel the cool breeze from the traffic, and she didn't feel trapped. An escape was within reach. Her heart still hammered against her throat, and she wished she had her shawl to wrap around her. All she wanted to do was hide somewhere.

Mai pulled her cell phone out of her purse and pulled up Stephanie's number. Staring at it, she didn't know what to do. Part of her wanted to scream at her friend, but she knew that Steph would never do anything deliberate to hurt her feelings. The date started out incredible. She never felt so pretty or special. Gaspar smiled and touched her hand so softly and insisted on getting them a bottle of champagne from the year she was born. It felt like a magical evening. But then he excused himself and when he came back, it all went to hell.

She dropped the phone back into her purse and stared out the window and felt the hot tears run down her cheeks as she finally started to calm down. If only she could have given him a piece of her mind. She should have stayed home and gotten some work done.

"Nice phone, lady."

Chapter Five

Brodie sat stretched out in his favorite chair with his arms tucked under his head, legs stretched out on the footrest. This recliner didn't match any of the furniture in the room. In fact, its brown corduroy material made it stick out like a sore thumb, but he knew his wife would never make him get rid of it. She knew he loved this chair, not to mention their daughter was conceived in this very spot. That memory made him grin, and he thought of calling his beautiful mate in here and seeing if he could talk her into another cub.

"Stephanie, where are you?"

Silence.

Brodie sat up and collapsed the footrest and listened for his wife. Getting up, he followed the sound of her pacing the floor of the back porch. Belle slept peacefully upstairs in her crib, so he knew that wasn't the problem. Although Steph tended to worry about strange things at times. She also spontaneously came up with ideas and followed through only to rethink her decisions later.

"Baby? Are you all right?"

Stephanie worried the edge of her thumbnail as she paced. The other held the phone. He quietly sniffed the air. *Oh shit, this was bad.* He stepped in front of her so she paced directly into his chest. "What happened, doll?"

"Um nothing?" She blinked up at him and tried to smile. "Mai had a date tonight, and she promised to call me and let me know everything went all right."

"Mai is on a date? That's great." He really like Stephanie's best friend. Mai cared deeply for those she considered family, but she was caught in a web of fear that only she could get herself out of. Not that it stopped his wife from trying to help in every way."

"Um yeah. I kinda set it up."

"You set her up on a blind date? With who?" Brodie knew damn well if he started to get agitated, his wife would feel it. Steph had a habit of overreacting at times, and right now she smelled like she was on the boarder of freaking out.

"I don't really know him, but he came highly recommended."

"Recommended?" Oh, this sounded like Steph followed through with one of her crazy ideas. "Okay, I take it you don't know this man?"

She shook her head and looked close to tears.

"Baby, you need to tell me what happened. I can feel your anxiety coming off you in waves. Belle will feel it, too, if you don't calm down soon." He scooped up into his arms and moved over to the large porch swing. Settling her in his lap, he rubbed her back. "Now start at the beginning and tell me everything."

"You're going to freak."

"No, I won't. I'll help you fix whatever has you worried."

"Mai needs someone in her life that will make her feel good about herself and help build her confidence. That is a tall order for one normal person. I thought about you having a big poker night for all your single friends, but I didn't want her to feel overwhelmed. And your friends tend to err on the side of overbearing."

"Not to mention that most of them aren't human."

"Yes, that's a big deal. I really hope you tell her the truth soon because I suck at keeping secrets.

Brodie smiled at her and pressed a kiss to the soft skin below her ear. "So where did you find a perfect date for Mai when you don't even know the man?" As soon as he said the words a thought blossomed in his head. *Oh please not that.*

"I hired a male escort to take Mai to lunch this afternoon, and she hasn't called me back yet."

"WHAT!"

"I knew you would freak!" Stephanie tried to push her way off his lap, but he held on to her.

"Baby, I don't think that was an overreaction. But how did you ever come up with this idea?"

"She needs a professional date. Someone who would make her feel good about herself. She needs this, only she isn't answering her phone, and you know she always has it on.

"Maybe the date is going really well?"

"He's a professional, Brodie. I paid for a lunch date. It's been eight hours and twenty minutes. She hasn't called. What if he hurt her?"

"What if they got distracted?"

"I didn't pay for that, and I told him not to. I'm not looking to get her laid. I want her confidence back!"

"All right. Give her a little more time, and if you haven't heard from her, then I'll go out and look."

"Oh, Brodie, I didn't mean for this to go so wrong."

"You don't know that it has." He kissed her on the forehead. His wife had the softest heart in the universe, and he was its protector.

"Why don't you give me the number of the man who you hired, and I'll call him? I'll be able to hear if anything is going on in the background, and I'll know if he is lying.

Stephanie straddled his hips and kissed him. "Thank you. I really screwed up this time, didn't I?"

"I know you meant the best, baby, but be prepared that Mai might not agree with you.

The phone rang in her hand at that moment. "Mai?" she asked as soon as she got it turned on. Brodie could hear the shake to Mai's voice from where he sat. It made all his protective instincts stand on end.

"What were you thinking, Stephanie! How could you do that to me?"

"Oh, I'm sorry, Mai. I wanted you to have a nice time out, and I wanted it to be perfect."

A sniffle sounded through the phone. "It was horrible."

"Mai, where are you? Brodie will come to get you, and I'm going to kill that worthless asshole myself."

Brodie swallowed the grin that pulled at the corners of his lips. His wife didn't swear much, but if her temper got up, she could peel paint from the walls with her voice.

"I'm on a pay phone in Union Station."

"Where is your phone?"

"I got mugged. They took my handbag, and I left my shawl at the restaurant. I'm all by myself, and everyone is staring."

Brodie stomped into his boots second later and grabbed a blanket to take with him in the truck. He was angry enough to kill right now. "Stephanie, tell Mai I'm on my way with the truck. I'll be there in fifteen minutes but stay on the on the phone with her, and I'll text you when she should come out front to meet me."

"Should she contact the police?" Brodie heard Mai's ask the question, but Stephanie had to repeat it so it looked convincing.

"I'll take her down and stay with her when she files a report. Tell her to stay put. I'm on my way." He pressed a quick kiss to his wife's temple. She gave him a watery smile. He knew she felt terrible for how everything turned out. His lovely bride always wanted everyone to be as happy as her.

* * * *

Brodie parked out front of Union Station and put on his flashers, which earned him a few angry honks from other drivers, but he didn't give a shit about them. Moments after texting his wife, Mai came out the front doors of Union Station. She practically ran across the wide sidewalk, her arms wrapped around herself. He jumped out of the truck with the blanket and opened her door for her. Mai hesitated for a moment as she got close. "Come here, Mai."

She walked into his arms and let him hug her. She felt like her entire core shook, and she sniffed against his chest. The unmistakable scent of wolf surrounded her and made the hair on Brodie's neck rise. Where did Mai run into a shifter? The dinner date or the mugger. If there was a rogue wolf in this city attacking women, Brodie would take care of the piece of shit himself.

He opened the blanket and wrapped it around her shoulders. "Come on, honey. Let's get you home."

"Thanks for coming to get me, Brodie." Mai stepped away and climbed into his truck. "I know it's a pain in the ass coming to get me."

"Honey, I have been friends with your brothers for years, and you are my wife's best friend. I will come and get you where ever and whenever you need."

Mai sniffed and looked out the window. He glanced over and rubbed her lightly on the arm. "How about we stop off at the station and you tell the police what happened?"

"I just want to go home."

"I understand that, sweetheart, but I really think you need to report this." He merged out into traffic and turned right onto Young to get on the QEW highway.

"I will tomorrow, I promise."

"Mai, did the mugger touch you at anytime? Grab your arm or get physical with you?" If the mugger was a rogue shifter, this would explain how she got the scent of wolf on her.

"No, never. He had a knife and flashed it in front of my face. I didn't even look up at him after that. I got a bit of a look at him, but not that good." He could smell the truth to her words, and that gave him a slight sense of relief. It also meant that his wife had the phone number of this wolf disguised as a dinner date. As soon as he got home, he was going to make a call.

"How about you stay at our house tonight? Stephanie feels horrible right now, and I know she wants to see for herself that you are all right."

"Please take me to my home, Brodie. I appreciate what you and Steph want to do, but I want to stay in my own bed tonight."

"All right." Brodie reached over and patted Mai's arm. He would have preferred to have her sit next to him and let him wrap his arm around her and make her feel safe again, but he knew she wouldn't let him. "Where are Jelani and Marcario these days?" Mai adored her brothers, and hopefully talking about them would make her feel better.

"Jelani is still traveling with Doctors Without Borders. He's been a Haiti for the past couple months. The locals adore him of course. Wherever he goes, everyone comes to see the doctors, but I think it's because he makes them laugh and forget the terrible things around them." She wiped at her eyes and pulled the blanket tighter around her. "Jelani is designing the building plans for some new schools and organizing having them built for almost no charge. He wants to make them as resistant to local weather patterns as possible."

"When did you see them last?"

"Not since Christmas when we all met in New York."

Brodie knew that Mai's family were very active in taking care of as many people in the world as possible, but spending the holidays in a hotel room and going out for dinner wasn't fun to him. "You're still going to come to our house this year right?"

"Um…maybe." Mai looked out the window and appeared to be watching the condos they passed. He could scent the untruth in her words and anger. Right now she was pissed as hell at Stephanie, and he couldn't blame her, but his wife meant well. Not wanting to bring it up, he decided to be quiet and drive. After a few minutes, Mai's breathing leveled out as she dozed off.

Brodie got Mai home safely and didn't leave until after he checked every one of her rooms to reassure her and himself. The wolf scent still clung to her, and that he found disturbing. It had to be because the jerk upset her so badly. Once her emotions settled, then the scent would go away as well.

*** *

"You hurt someone under my protection tonight. I have every right to call you to claw, and I'm not entirely certain why I shouldn't. Fucking wolves."

There was a loaded pause on the line before the man spoke again. "What are you talking about?"

"Don't play stupid with me, puppy. I know Mai's scent almost as well as my mate's. She came here tonight reeking of wolf."

"She's all right?" Brodie could hear the authenticity of the other man's concern in his voice. "I tried to look for her but lost her in traffic. I wanted to explain. There was a huge misunderstanding."

"Really, well then next time I suggest you be more careful with your dates. This misunderstanding would cost you your life if I had my way."

"I am going to let that threat slide since I am in the wrong, but don't think I am a beta about to roll over and show you my belly. You try that and you'll find yourself on the receiving end of some claws yourself."

"Bring it on, boy. I have been around a lot of shifters in my time. I don't submit to anyone."

"A solitary, huh? In this country, I would suspect an ursul perhaps?"

"Stay away from me and mine or you'll find out first hand."

Brodie could hear a vicious growl in the background and almost expected to hear the phone flying through the air. "Who's pacing the floor next to you? Is that the bastard that tore into her?"

"As I tried to explain, it was all a terrible misunderstanding. I didn't make my intentions clear, and the wrong assumptions were made."

"What, is his nose broken as well?"

"Frankly, yes." Another violent snarl could be heard over the line.

"You think I can't hear your brother growling from here. Tell him to stop that, or I'll tear his throat out with my claws."

Despite his threat, Brodie could understand his being pissed off. He wouldn't like it either if someone told his secrets. The fact that Gaspar decided to share his brother's weakness told him much about how bad he felt.

"Please, let me talk to her and try to explain it to her."

"No. She doesn't know anything of our world, and I don't see why she should."

"That isn't your choice to make, ursul."

"But it's made. You will stay away from those under my protection."

"You will not keep our mate from us!"

Brodie could feel his jaw drop. *Oh, shit, shit, shit.* No wonder that lupine scent clung to her like that. *Oh, bloody hell, this entire situation is taking a swirly of momentous proportions.*

"If this is the way you treat your mate, then it's best that you stay away from her."

A gasp in the doorway drew his attention. He glanced over to see his wife standing there with both hands over her mouth. He held a finger to his lips, hoping to ensure her silence. Stephanie's eyes looked as wide as saucers, and she mouthed the word "mate."

"We will make it up to her. I swear. Please."

"We?"

"My brother and I are twins."

"Identical, I take it?" Brodie had a very good idea what was going on now. He gripped the top of his nose between his fingers. "Fuck boys, you know how to make a situation worse."

"That's your opinion. I am asking you to let us have another chance."

"Let me talk to Mai first."

"It's not for you to tell. It is our right to confide the truth to her. You tell her now and she might run."

"Then you and your stuffed up nose for a brother would have to hunt her."

"And if someone told your mate before you had a chance? Would you have wanted to hunt her?"

Brodie knew that was a loaded question. Stephanie led him on a merry chase before he caught up to her. One too many pranks and she finally fell into his paws. Thankfully, his incredible mate accepted the entire situation with her normal graciousness. She screamed like a banshee and punched him in the face. Feeling that impact made him feel like the world opened up like an oyster because if she was angry enough to hit him, that meant she didn't fear him. He swore to never let her go after that.

"All right, boys. You want her? You'll need earn her trust and her love. You fuck up like this again and I'll shred you both into small enough pieces to feed the damn squirrels in my backyard for a month."

He hung up the phone and turned to his wife. "Only you, Stephanie, would managed to set your best friend up on the worst date in the universe only to discover later that her blind dates are her mates."

"Oh my goodness, what are we going to tell her?"

Brodie moved across the room and caught his luscious wife in his arms before she had a chance to bolt to her friend. "We, my dear sweet pudding pop, are not going to tell her anything."

She wriggled in his arms, making his cock thicken. He loved the bit of weight she had put on since Belle was born. It made her softer and more of an armful. Her boobs were bigger now, too, and he couldn't put into words how much he enjoyed that.

"Brodie, pay attention."

"I am," he lied, still thinking about how delicious she tasted when he licked the sensitive skin under her breasts. A small hand gripped his jaw and forced him to look up.

"I'm speaking to you, bear boy."

"I'm not a boy, little girl. I can prove it, too." He stepped over to the wall and pressed her up against it, angling his hips so that the apex of her legs rode along his length. Stephanie's eyes fluttered, and a soft moan escaped her lips. "You're trying to distract me."

"Not completely." Brodie wanted to plunge himself deep within her. The bond they shared echoed both of their sensations. "I'm trying to have sex with my perfect mate."

Her laugh sounded like happiness personified. "Okay, you win."

"No telling Mai. Let her find out on her own. If they are really mates, then it's up to them to fix their fuck-up."

"I don't want her hurt, Brodie. I feel like I need to protect her."

"Your mama bear instincts are getting stronger, only you have included Mai in with Belle. She's an adult, baby, and you need to step back on this one. Be her friend, be there when she needs a shoulder and I'll be there if she needs someone's ass kicked, but other than that it's up to them to sort this out. Would you have wanted someone to interfere with us?"

"No, I guess not." She wriggled against his length, the dampness soaking through her panties. "I don't think anyone is interfering with us now."

"No my precious mate. No one is. It's you and me forever."

"The two and a half bears." Steph grinned. His wife had the oddest sense of humor, but he wouldn't change her for the world. "Now papa bear, what is this I heard about you being too hard?"

Chapter Six

Mai stalked the length of her apartment. Pacing back and forth, her head hurt from the tears, not all of them because of Gaspar turning into the biggest asshole on the planet or that she had been mugged. Not long ago her instincts were better, but not anymore. She could feel her life slipping out of her control. Maybe she should take the pills the doctor ordered. If she walked around like a zombie, wouldn't that be better than the alternative?

Sitting down at her computer, she looked over rental properties north of the city. She needed to get away, far away, from the city and everything. Now that she was out of work, she needed to downgrade and get away from the expense of city life. She knew her savings could hold her over for a while, but it wouldn't last long. At least now she was going to have a lot of time to concentrate on her web designs, but who the hell would hire her?

Her cell phone chirped catching her attention. A quick glance at it revealed Steph's number. So far her best friend had phoned every fifteen minutes, and Mai hadn't answered. She knew that Steph didn't mean any harm. She never did. And hiring a professional was a clever idea and had Mai thought of it herself, she might have tried it. She didn't want to think of that afternoon and her crazy, wild, incredible time in the forest with Gaspar. She ran her fingers through her hair and tried not to think that he had been paid to fuck her. That is what made her feel sick, the idea that someone would need to be paid to have sex with her. How could something that seemed so magical turn so incredibly wrong so quickly?

The knock at the door startled her. *Must be food.* She ordered a bunch from her favorite Thai place down the road. Ordering lots ensured she would have some leftovers for a couple meals. She moved over to the door and looked out the peephole. Gaspar stood across the hallway, her favorite silk shawl in one hand and what looked to be a large doughnut box from Tim Horton's with a tray holding a couple coffees in the other. Mai's heart jumped into her throat. Perhaps she could be very quiet and he wouldn't know she was here, and then he would leave. Hopefully, he left her shawl behind. She didn't want to have anything to do with him.

Except that he looked very uncertain and so damn cute. *What's wrong with you? The man's a total douche bag!* A damn good-looking one. He looked down and then up at the peephole, directly at her.

"Mai, I really sorry. Please, let me explain."

Mai didn't move. Part of her desperately wanted to let him in. She wanted to badly to curl up in his arms, which was totally ridiculous because the man proved himself to be a total jerk.

"I know you're there, Mai." He pointed down to the bottom of her door. "I can see your shadow."

Mai looked down at her feet and back at the lights behind her. *Crap.* So that's how Brodie always knew when she stood looking out the door. She placed both chains on her door before opening it.

Peeking around the door, she looked up at Gaspar and held out her hand. "My shawl?"

"Mai, please let me in. I really would like the opportunity to explain what happened. I mean…" Gaspar handed her the delicate shawl and then ran and hand through his hair, pushing it back, but it immediately slipped forward again. "I'm really sorry. Your friend told me how you like your coffee." He held up the tray holding two cups.

He looked so sweet standing there. Her brain remembered the hurt his words caused, but her body had a mind of its own at the moment. A distinct tingle ran down her spine, and she could feel her nipples tightening. Dammit and here she was in nothing but a T-shirt and jeans.

"You spoke to Steph?"

Gaspar nodded and winced slightly.

"Let me guess, she threatened to disembowel you with a spoon?"

"At the very least. She's very creative when she's pissed off, but I'm not here because of that. I called her to ask for your address so I could apologize properly."

Well, if he called Steph, then she would know he planned to come over here. She nodded and then closed the door to unchain it. Opening the door again. Gaspar didn't rush ahead. He waited until she stepped aside. "All right, come in, Gaspar."

Gaspar stepped into her small apartment, and instantly Mai felt like it shrunk three times its size. He carried such a presence that he filled every space in here. No matter what, she would always remember his being here. She wrapped her shawl around her shoulders, covering her T-shirt and her body's reaction to having him so close to her.

"First thing, my name isn't Gaspar."

"Oh yea, I guess you guys have a different name when you are working."

"Well, yes and no." He held out his hand. "My name is Vencel Sofalvi. Gaspar is my brother."

"I don't understand." She shook his hand, an automatic reaction to his offer.

Both of them opened the tab on their coffee, and he spoke as she took her first sip.

"Gaspar had an emergency come up that night, and he needed my help."

"So do you often sleep with women for him?"

"No, it's not like that. Gaspar gave up that side of his work a long time ago. He is a strictly a companion now, and he's good at it."

"Yes, he is." Mai didn't bother to add *and you're not,* but by the look on his face, she got her point across. What she didn't understand is why he had sex with her if that wasn't part of his normal routine.

* * * *

"Can we sit down?"

"Um, yes, of course." Mai plunked herself into a chair and tucked her long legs up under her.

"Did you want a doughnut?"

Mai accepted the box from him and lifted the lid to see what kinds he brought. "There are a dozen strawberry blossoms in here. Steph told you, didn't she?"

"That they are your favorite and I should show up with a dozen and a large double double and be on my knees when you open the door? Nope, she didn't say anything of the sort."

Mai couldn't help but smile at Vencel because that did sound exactly like something Steph would say. He smiled back, and she questioned again what a man this good looking was doing standing in her apartment. She placed her coffee on a side table and then sat back in her overstuffed chair and bit into the fancy bit of pastry.

"I really acted like an obnoxious asshole, Mai. I jumped to conclusions without thinking first and said some really awful things."

"Well, it's not like they weren't true."

"Regardless, you didn't know, and I had no business being an arrogant prick. I'm really very sorry."

"It's all right." She started feeling bad for him, Vencel really looked apologetic for his behavior, and Mai didn't like to carry a grudge anyways. It wasn't like he was responsible for what happened after she left.

"You friend did say something else I thought was strange. She told me I should ask you what happened to your phone that night. Did you leave it at the restaurant? Because I didn't see it when I picked up your shawl."

The doughnut turned into what tasted like ash in her mouth. She placed the rest of it on a napkin on the arm of her chair and took a sip of her coffee. Her stomach turned over at the memory of that night. Mai didn't want to tell him about being mugged. That would be like rubbing salt into an open wound, no doubt Stephanie's plan. But, Vencel looked remorseful enough that she didn't want to think of that moment on the streetcar again. Besides, it's not like he was her protector or anything. Nobody took care of her but her and sometimes Brodie and Stephanie.

"There really isn't anything to tell. I lost it when I ran out of the restaurant. I snuck out the back patio, and there is an alley back there."

"You went down an alley at night? You could have been hurt. I wish you had rather thrown your glass of champagne at me and then stormed out the front."

"I was fine. It's a short walk, and then I cut up to the street and caught a streetcar back to Union Station. Nothing to it."

She turned in the chair and tucked both her feet to the side, trapping her hands between her knees so he wouldn't notice they started shaking. She felt overheated and queasy, an icy feeling shot down her spine, and she felt a true fear that she might have to fight a panic attack in her own home. If she couldn't be safe here, then where could she be?

"Mai, Gaspar and I would really like another opportunity to take you out to dinner. We would both like to."

"You don't have to do that." The thought of going out with them made her throat close up. There was no way she could go there or anywhere with him.

"Yes, we want to. It's the least we can do for ruining your night."

"I know that Steph paid you, and your brother might feel a certain obligation..."

"Gaspar returned the money right after he dropped you off at home, and we are asking you out on a date."

Mai wanted to think that it didn't make a difference, but knowing that there was no money involved did ease her mind. "This is all really strange. I mean, you're asking me on his behalf?"

"He's outside." Vencel pointed to the window. "Parked across the street in the silver truck."

"Huh?" Mai pushed herself out of the chair and stepped to the window. Glancing back, she reassured herself that he stayed sitting. Looking out the window proved he wasn't lying. A big truck parked on the side of the road with a man that looked identical to Vencel sitting at the wheel. A small light shone up at his face. He must have been texting or playing a game. "Why didn't he come up with you?"

"I wanted to come up here first and beg forgiveness. Also, we didn't want to overwhelm you with the twin thing right away."

Gaspar looked up at the window and waved at her. She automatically gave him a small wave back.

"Can he come up, too, Mai?"

"All right." She started to wave at him to come up, but Gaspar was already getting out of the truck and heading across the street. She watched the way he walked. Both brothers moved with such grace. "How did he know?"

"I messaged him." Vencel held up his phone before setting it down on the table. "Mai, I want you to understand that I didn't ask you out for Gaspar. I asked you out to dinner with both of us."

He looked at her expectantly, and Mai knew she was missing something important. "Okay, you want me to go out with you both. That's no....oh." She felt her cheeks burn at the thought that crossed her mind. It was the mental image of her between the two of them in the forest that quickly followed that made her blush.

"We're incredibly close, even for twins. I didn't want you to misunderstand my intentions." He walked across the room as he spoke and opened her door as Gaspar reached it.

Seeing both of them side by side made her heart skip a beat. She hadn't slept with Vencel, so it wasn't in the forefront of her mind when they spoke, but as soon as Gaspar entered the room, she recalled every moment against the tree in vivid clarity.

Gaspar prowled toward her. There was no other way to explain how he moved. "Mai, I swear I never meant for you to be hurt." Before she could say anything, he wrapped his hand around the back of her neck and bent his head, kissing her as if he hadn't seen her in years. She felt light-headed and grasped his shoulders as he was her only anchor in a raging storm.

She blinked, trying to clear her thoughts when he lifted his head and caressed the back of her cheek with his knuckles. "*Szia, Angyalom*...hello my angel."

Vencel cleared his throat. "I hope you will look at me like that one day, Mai."

"Subtle as always, Vencel?" Gaspar grinned down at her. "I've missed you."

Mai glanced between the two of them feeling a bit overwhelmed. She stepped back from Gaspar's grasp and pulled her shawl closer around her shoulders. "I don't know why you would."

"And for that I cannot apologize enough."

Mai moved away from the both of them, needing some space to think. Standing so close, all she could think about was Gaspar putting her up against her apartment wall while his brother watched.

"Did she tell you what happened to her phone?" Gaspar looked at her, but his words were obviously meant for his brother.

"I'll let you explain, Mai." Vencel smiled at her from his position on the couch. His legs stretched out in front of him, one arm stretched across the back.

"It's gone, and I don't know why the two of you are so concerned about my phone." Mai got up and took the box of doughnuts to the small counter in her kitchen.

"*Nyuszikam.*"

Gaspar eyed her suspiciously. "She does act like one sometimes."

"What's that mean? I act like what?" Mai tried to take the edge out of her voice, but even she heard it.

"A little rabbit." Vencel watched her from over the back of the couch, and Gaspar leaned against the wall following her every movement. "Running away from the first sign of trouble."

"I'm not running anywhere."

"Mai, seriously, what's the big deal? Why lie about it?"

Their pestering her was starting to piss her off. Why couldn't they leave her alone already? She could kick them out, but then part of her didn't want to be alone. *I need to start taking those pills the doctor gave me since I'm obviously going insane.*

"I don't understand why you won't take my word for it and drop it. I don't need either of you to buy me a phone." She was going to throttle her meddling friend forever saying anything to them.

"You're acting like you lied, but I can't understand why you would."

Mai threw the cloth on the counter and snapped at them both. "Because I got mugged. I had a knife flashed in front of my face, and he told me to hand over my phone and purse."

Both Gaspar and Vencel stared at her like statues, each with identical expressions of shock on their faces. Her throat stung, and she knew that tears wouldn't be far behind. "I don't think I feel like company after all. I remembered I have a big program to write, and I need to start. You two should both please go."

"*Jajjls ienem!*" Vencel dropped his head back on the couch and pressed the heels of his hands to his eyes. "I can't forgive myself for this one." In a blur of moment, Gaspar swooped her into his arms and hugged her close to his body. "Oh god, Mai. I'm sorry. We're both sorry."

Mai sank into his embrace. She wanted to be mad at them, but a feeling of rightness washed over her, as if this was where she was meant to be. "It's all right, Gaspar. There was nothing either of you could have done."

"But because we weren't upfront and honest with you, everything went wrong."

Mai quickly swiped a tear from her cheek when she felt it escape. "I was scared, but I'm all right now."

"You're lying again, stop it."

"I am not, and how would you know anyway?" She pushed at his shoulder, feeling a bit embarrassed by her reaction and her imagination. "Really, I'm okay. Other than a big scare, nothing happened."

Gaspar pressed a kiss to the top of her head. "We will make it up to you."

"I don't need either of you to do anything."

Gaspar kissed her temple and then her ear sending shivers down her arms. He inhaled deeply right at her neck, and she immediately leaned back. "What are you doing?"

"Did you get him?" Vencel came around the couch to where they stood.

Gaspar looked up and shook his head.

"Get who? What are you talking about?" She looked back and forth between them. If she didn't know better, she would have bet they were speaking to each other but not saying a word.

Gaspar looked down at her, looking seriously concerned. "Is that really all, Mai? You didn't get cut or anything else?"

"No, not at all. I made it down to Union, and Brodie came to get me and brought me home." The men looked at each other and again Mai couldn't decipher what the look meant.

Vencel came up behind her and rested his hands on her shoulders. Rubbing her arms, he stood so close that she felt his chest against her back. What did occur to her was that standing here with both their arms around her she didn't feel panicky anymore. The clammy feeling and tightness in her throat drifted away leaving behind a calm she thought she'd never feel again.

"I'm going to replace your phone, Mai."

She looked over her shoulder, twisting in their embrace to do so. "It's okay, you don't have to."

"I know, but I want to." He brushed his lips against hers, leaving behind the same feeling of shimmering sparkles on her skin that Gaspar made her feel. "You and I are going to go out and you pick whichever one you want." She would have argued with him, but he looked so serious, she wondered if he would drag her out anyways if she tried to cancel. He ran his fingers through the hair at her temple. "Or you can pick one out online, either way you're comfortable works for me.

A heavy knock at the door interrupted her before she could argue anymore about the phone. "Good, food's here. We can talk and eat."

They acted as if she didn't say anything about telling them to go. "Didn't I tell you two to leave?"

Both the men froze, and Vencel brushed his knuckles against her cheek. "We will if you want us to, Mai, but we would really like to stay for a bit longer."

"Well, I always order lots, and it's best when it's hot." She smiled slightly, glad they were going to stay. She couldn't explain why, but she really didn't want them to leave. It wasn't only because she already spent so much time alone. Deep inside, she felt an ache at the thought of them leaving her.

Both the guys smiled, obviously relieved. Mai noticed they each had a dimple in the middle of one cheek. The opposite cheek for each of them. With the few days' growth of hair on their faces, she never would have noticed if she hadn't been standing so close.

Gaspar got the door, and Vencel helped Mai grab plates and forks. While they unpacked the food, she had Gaspar open a bottle of wine she was saving.

* * * *

Gaspar could hardly eat. He fluctuated from feeling horrendously guilty for what happened to Mai, to feeling like he wanted to grab her by the hips and dive his face between her legs. Now that she relaxed, her simmering arousal was like a beacon for his senses. He could tell everything she felt, especially strong feelings pounding against him. Her laughter might as well have been a silk cloth stroking his cock.

I can hear your thoughts from here, and I feel the same way. She is incredible, but I wish she was a bit stronger.

She's stronger than she gives herself credit for. Her lack of faith in herself might be the root of all this.

His brother's thoughts quieted, which meant he seriously considered Gaspar's words. He knew Vencel normally stayed away from women he deemed as weak. After how many women they saw killed in the war, he could understand Vencel's thinking. His brother felt each needless death deeply, and it created a deep fear within him.

He took a sip of his Italian wine and enjoyed the tangy fruit that complimented the spices in the Thai food. Mai sipped on her second glass of wine, and he could see her relax a bit more in their presence. What would it take for her to show them her bedroom? Vencel excused himself to go to the washroom, disappearing down the hall.

"Gaspar, can I ask you something personal?" She picked at her food and then put her plate down and picked up her wine glass.

He put his plate on the coffee table next to hers, having a good idea what subject was about to come up. It was only a matter of time before she asked, and he'd rather get it out of the way sooner than later. "You can ask me anything. In fact, I want you to ask."

"Do you like being an escort?"

"There was a time when, yes, I did. But, the reasons for doing it in the first place don't matter anymore." *Because I've found you.*

"So why keep doing it."

"I'm not. As of two days ago I retired." She gave him a suspicious glare over her wine glass. If she didn't believe him now, she would eventually. "Really, just like that?"

"It served its purpose and helped to pay the bills."

"Did you ever feel bad being someone getting paid to have sex?"

"No, because I was always my own boss and never fell into the trap that so many others do in this line of work. Some people fall into this out of desperation and then can't get out of it. I always had my brother there to keep my priorities straight."

Her bed isn't anywhere near big enough for the three of us.

Gaspar would have laughed at Vencel's disgusted tone if he didn't feel so frustrated. He picked up his plate and continued to eat while planning out how to proceed. He couldn't simply announce that she was their mate and they wanted her to move in with them.

Mai placed her wine glass on the table and picked her plate up again. She didn't say anything, lost in her own thoughts. He knew this would be a lot for her to take in, but how could he explain that working as an escort allowed him to meet as many women as possible in his hunt for their mate? Vencel might not have agreed with his methods, but he couldn't argue with the results.

"How long have you lived here, Mai?" Vencel asked as he stepped back into the room. Mai looked up, and Gaspar took the opportunity to top off her glass again.

She turned quickly and pointed a finger at him. "Stop putting more wine in my glass when you think I'm not looking." It didn't stop her from taking another swallow before answering his brother.

He knew she had a strong spirit buried inside her and thrilled at the sight of it. If she wasn't feeling comfortable with them, she wouldn't have said anything. He wouldn't mind her leaning against him for support, but his brother needed to see her inner strength. She couldn't be more perfect for them.

"About six years. I rented it in my last year at U of T. I've thought about moving, but this is a rent controlled building, and it seems like so much work to move all my computer stuff when I have it set up here just the way I like it."

"Where would you move if you could have a choice?"

"Up north. My friends have a cottage up near Georgian Bay, and I love going up there. I can work on my web designs anywhere, and the cost of living is so much cheaper anywhere outside Toronto. I'm tired of living in the city and would prefer somewhere slower paced.

"What about Huntsville?" Gaspar met his brother's gaze for a moment. He could see the hesitation in Vencel's expression. His brother couldn't scent what he could and still harbored doubt that Mai was meant to be theirs.

"Huntsville? That's up near Algonquin isn't it? I don't know much about the area."

"We have a house a little east of there, on Ecstasy Lake. It's close enough to come to the city for work, and we have a condo here when we need to stay for longer than a day trip."

"You know, you should come up there." Vencel offered, surprising Gaspar. "It would give you a chance to look at some properties that might interest you."

"I might do that. Do you know of any good real estate agents and hotels?"

"Yes to both, but you won't be staying in one. You can stay with us for a long as you like. We have a guest bedroom you are welcome to. Vencel and I would be happy to chauffer you all over wherever you want to go."

"You don't have to do that. I don't want to be a bother."

He could scent the concern written all over her face. As much as he and his wolf wanted her in his bed, he didn't want to scare her off.

"That is the last thing you will ever be, Mai. Why not take a couple days off and check out the area for yourself? Then if you decide you want to see a few places, we can arrange it." Gaspar tried very hard to be diplomatic with his words when he wanted to simply tell her that she would be going up north. As their mate, her place was with them. He couldn't protect her if he didn't know where she ran off to.

"*Nyuszikam*, there is no obligations for you to do anything but come up and enjoy our hospitality." Vencel gave Gaspar a pointed look, and he knew what his brother wanted to make her understand.

"You are more than welcome in our home and our bed." Mai jerked slightly and her cheeks turned a lovely shade of pink again. She looked, wide-eyed, between him and his bother. "But we're going to be incredibly honest with you because we don't want any more misunderstandings. Vencel and I share everything, *Angyalom*."

Chapter Seven

Vencel and I share everything...

Mai heard Gaspar's words replayed a thousand times in her memory over the next forty-eight hours. She wanted to think that didn't have any influence on her borrowing Steph's car and traveling up to their home, but it did. Mai enjoyed their company the other night. They ate and talked, and neither of them pushed her after revealing their intentions. They didn't do anything more than touch her arm or hold her hand, and by the end of the night she was ready to invite them to her bed. But, all that happened was they each gave her a knee-quaking kiss before leaving that night.

Since her arrival at their house this morning, neither man said anything about her sharing their bed. They were polite and kind, driving her around Huntsville and the surrounding area. They looked at a few apartments and houses for rent. But there weren't that many to choose from. Ecstasy Lake only offered on small hotel that catered to tourists. It didn't dampen her spirits through. Everything smelled beautiful up here, away from the smog and stagnant air of the city. Even the food tasted better up here.

Gaspar barbequed up a delicious dinner, and again she was treated to gentle caresses and stolen kisses over the evening. Vencel played with her hair as he told her a bit about the history of Ecstasy Lake, and Gaspar often touched her arm as he spoke to her. Innocent contacts on their own, but added up over the evening and she was ready to crawl out of her own skin. She felt as though she was a toy wound up too tight. All day she waited for something to happen, but it looked as though they were determined to keep their word not to make her feel obligated.

Obligation was the last thing she felt at the moment. She felt as though her tank top was made from horsehair, the mattress too hard, the pillow too soft. Everything felt irritating, and to top it off she was afraid to do anything about it. *Fear again.* Mai thumped the pillow for a twentieth time and flipped over to her other side, feeling angry. Always it was fear that ruled her life and made her miss out on things that other people took for granted. Why couldn't she act out in a spontaneous manner and do something exciting?

Dammit, *why didn't she?* She sat up in bed and threw the sheet off herself. She was going to march out into the hall and then do something. She didn't know exactly what, but she would wing it. Before she lost her nerve, Mai left her room and went straight to the door across the hall and knocked lightly on it.

The door whipped open, revealing a gorgeous man in nothing but a pair of boxer briefs. A smile curled his lips, revealing the deep dimple in his left cheek. Mai opened her mouth to say something, but her voice froze in her throat.

"Come here, sweetheart." Vencel caught her hand, stepping backward to his bed. She willingly followed, uncertain what he had in mind. Sure her brain could come up with a dozen different scenarios for what might happen, but she couldn't be certain what they wanted. What if she wasn't any good and disappointed them?

Vencel scooted back against the headboard. "Little closer, *Nyuszikam.*" He tilted his head slightly as he looked at her face, "What is going on in that head of yours?"

"Nothing, I'm good."

She felt the bed move behind her and her heart rate ratcheted up in speed. A quick glance over her shoulder revealed that Gaspar followed her movements. Vencel placed a hand gently on her cheek and lead her gaze back to him. "I can sense what you're feeling, Mai, but I don't understand why."

Gaspar flopped down on the bed next to her leg. "You need to talk to us, Mai. We're not mind readers."

"Are you sure about that? Because sometimes I think that's exactly what you're doing."

Vencel sat up and pressed his lips against her neck. "We're very good at reading body language and picking up subtle clues. I know you're excited about being here right now, but something is bothering you."

"If you aren't ready for both of us, then we can wait." Gaspar slid his large hand over her hip and stroked her lower back. "But you are ready, aren't you?"

"Yes." Mai heard the words leave her lips before she could think. "No...I mean...I don't know if I can make you both happy."

"I can assure you that we are both deliriously happy right now." Vencel's breath tickled her neck as he spoke. She shivered, and he wrapped his hands around the backs of her arms sliding them up to her shoulders. "Cold?"

She shook her head. Gaspar pressed a kiss to her hipbone. *When did he move that close?*

"Tell us what's bothering you."

Her body felt tingly all over, and every time she tried to formulate a reasonable excuse, it scattered. She wasn't a virgin, but never had she felt as in tune with any other lover. Never did she imagine ever trying to satisfy more than one man at a time.

"Mai," Vencel's deep voice whispered in her ear, his tongue flicking at the edge of her lobe.

"Tell us." Gaspar licked a sensitive spot next to her hipbone, and she blurted out the truth.

"I'm not good at this." Her body arched slightly, despite her brain trying to maintain some control over herself. Vencel's hands rested on her shoulders, and Gaspar's hands roamed all over her hips and back. "...not good enough to take you both on."

A low growl vibrated against her waist making her jump. Before she could look down, Vencel leaned back and cupped her jaw with his large hands. She blinked at the anger she saw in his gaze. *What did I do wrong?*

"Stop tearing yourself down. It's pissing me off." His firm grip relaxed slightly, but he wouldn't let her look when she felt Gaspar shift and move off the bed. "Where's Gaspar going? I'm sorry, I didn't mean to hurt anyone's feelings. I can't choose between you."

"Who said you would have to?"

"No one, but you make my mind spin when you touch me. He does, too, and what if I don't give one of you enough attention?"

She instinctively felt a rushing behind her, and Gaspar's voice rumbled in her ear a moment later. *How did he move so quickly?* "Jealously? That's what you're worried about?"

"Why are you so surprised by that?" He nipped at the back of her neck and along her shoulder. The sharp nips stung but not in a painful way. Instead, they sent waves of sensation throughout her body.

"Mai, that is the last thing you have to worry about. If Gaspar and I have a problem, then we will sort it out, but never think for a moment that you're the cause."

"I don't know how that's possible."

"Because you don't know us that well yet, but you will." Vencel shifted, pressing up against her, reminding her that she was sitting high on his thighs. He cupped her ass and slid her forward until her core rested over him. His cock felt like a burning brand against her sensitized tissues. She had never been so wet, and they had hardly touched her. She tried to tilt her pelvis to get a more direct pressure against her clit, but Vencel's hands wouldn't let her move. Gaspar's hand slid around her chest, stroking the skin under her breasts. She arched her back against him, pressing her breasts forward. Wanting…any touch to relieve the pressure building within.

"Can you feel how hard I am, Mai?" Vencel shifted her slightly, and she slid across length of his cock. "You did this. Having you here naked in my lap is enough to make me hard enough to bang nails."

"He's not the only one." Gaspar took one of her hands in his and led it to the small of her back. There he pressed his erection against it. Mai curled her fingers around the girth and felt his cock slide up and down along her fingers. "Touching you is enough to make me want to explode. How can you imagine you aren't enough for both of us?"

Mai felt dizzy. She wanted to move so badly, to touch, and kiss them. "Let me touch you as well."

"Both of us, Mai?" Gaspar's whisper tickled the hair next to her neck.

"Don't leave again." Mai tried to slouch in Gaspar's embrace and force his hands up over her breasts. He laughed at her attempt but didn't move his hands. "I wasn't planning on it, sweetheart, I needed a moment to get myself better under control."

She opened her eyes and met Vencel's gaze. He must have seen something in her own that convinced him that she felt more confident, and she did. In their arms, she felt as if she could do anything.

The dark voices whispered concerns of having a panic attack here and now. Her heart rate stuttered, and her skin cooled at the prospect of the coming fear. She closed her eyes and hoped that she could pretend nothing was wrong.

A menacing growl snapped her out of the spiral that started to suck her under. Her attention snapped to the man in front of her, his teeth bared, his upper lip quivering slightly. "Pay attention to what we are doing to you, Mai." He lifted her to her knees and off his heated flesh. She whimpered slightly at the loss of contact. Gaspar's hands gripped her hips, supporting her. Vencel's fingers replaced Gaspar's on the skin below her breasts and then slid up to cup her. The heat from his fingers warmed her skin, and he ran his thumbs over her tight nipples. The direct contact sent an electrical shiver through her body, and she gasped for a breath.

"Watch me, Mai." Vencel's eyes almost looked luminescent in the fading light. She watched as he leaned forward and flicked one of her nipples with his tongue, sucking on the tight bud, then licked a path to the other side and repeated the movement. Mai couldn't believe how incredible it felt to watch him. His eyes almost glowed, and for a brief second, she thought they changed, but it had to be a trick of the light.

She almost forgot about Gaspar behind her, but he licked a path along the cleft of her ass, making her jump a second time. Vencel smiled, and then glanced down at her breasts to lave one of her nipples with his tongue before sucking it into his hot mouth and flicking it mercilessly. Watching Vencel cup her breasts while teasing her was one of the most erotic things she had ever seen, coupled with the nips and licks Gaspar spread over her lower back and across her ass.

Mai felt as if she might explode into a white-hot fireball. In an attempt to press her body against both men, she ended up stretched like a well-stroked cat.

"Oh, that's it, Mai." Vencel leaned backward against the bed, taking her with him, only Gaspar kept a hold of her hips so she ended up face down in a pile of pillows. Vencel held her to his mouth as he continued to worship her breasts, but now her pussy was completely exposed to Gaspar behind her. She could feel his breath on her thighs, but he wouldn't touch her. She wriggled and tried to push backward, but his hands kept her in place. "Gaspar." She whispered his name, needing him to touch her. She could feel moisture gathering at the apex of her legs, until finally spilling over. A drop ran along her thigh until she felt Gasper's tongue trace a path upward to catch it.

"Such a tasty treat." His voice trembled against her leg as he traced a line up her thigh.

"Oh please…"

"Sweet Mai. Tell me what you want."

She cried out in frustration, wanting to touch herself but knowing he wouldn't let her.

"Is he teasing you, Mai?"

"Yes, make him stop."

Gaspar stroked the backs of her thighs, but not where she needed it the most. A strong shudder ran along her limbs, she needed...needed.

"You don't want to do that, brother."

He softly brushed against her core, and Mai cried out at the exquisite pleasure that spiked through her. "Our woman is dripping with need here. I can't get enough of her scent or taste. Fuck me, Vencel, she tastes like creamed honey."

Vencel licked a path from Mai's breasts to her neck. Tracing a muscle along her shoulder, he bit down on the tendon and another shudder raked through Mai's body. *How did he know exactly where to do that?*

"I want a taste, Mai." She nodded, expecting him to slide lower and taste her. She might not survive it. The mere thought of one of them licking at her wet pussy sent her desire spiraling. "Give me your hand."

"What?" Mai looked down confused at the odd request. Vencel lay on his back beneath her holding out his hand. She braced herself on her elbow and placed her hand in his. He wrapped his hand around hers.

"Now touch yourself, *Nyuszikam*. Get your fingers nice and wet for me. She dropped her forehead to his shoulder and reached down between her legs. She wasn't going to last.

"That's it, sweet Mai. Show me how you like to be touched." Knowing that Gaspar lay there watching her should have embarrassed the hell out of her, but instead it turned her on even more. She gently stroked the swollen fold before slipping between. Even she was amazed at how wet she felt. Her fingers immediately arrowed in for her clit. Drawing circles around the little bud sent her rushing toward ecstasy. She teetered on the edge, her body shaking, demanding relief. One more stoke was all she needed.

"Oh no you don't." Vencel grabbed her hand before she could get any closer.

Mai cried out in frustration. So close, one more stroke, and she would have hurtled over the edge. She wanted to smack Vencel for denying her but instead found herself transfixed with the sight of him licking her fingers clean. He sucked her middle finger, the one she used to stroke her clit, deep into his mouth. His tongue ran over the length. He sucked again, and she could feel the pull on her clit as if it was in his mouth. "You taste like ambrosia."

"It's better directly from the source. " Gaspar's tongue stroked her from clit to the core. The sensations, too powerful to contain, made her cried out.

"Oh, please fuck me. Both of you, please, I can't stand it anymore."

"Now that is the honesty I was hoping to hear from you." Vencel finished cleaning her fingers off before helping her move back over his cock.

Mai ground herself down against his length, her hand pressed against Vencel's chest. He jerked up almost dislodging her. "Yes, oh yes." She tilted her hips, sliding her cream along his shaft.

"Fuck, Mai. Slow down. You're going to have me exploding before I ever get inside you." Vencel gripped her hips in his large hands. "Jesus, Gaspar, please tell me you're ready."

"Hell yeah. Here, *Angyalom*," Gaspar pressed a condom package into Mai's hand. Put that on him, Mai. Take your time if you want. He needs to learn some patience."

Mai couldn't help the laugh the bubbled up from deep inside her. Gaspar's bit of humor was lost on Vencel. Vencel tended to be a bit more intense and focused. Maybe that was the point his brother tried to make.

"Get that damn thing on me."

"Oh, I will." Mai wrapped her fingers around his length and stroked his length. Swiping her finger over his weeping tip she brought it to her mouth and licked it off. Vencel growled low in his throat. *Damn, that almost sounded real.* His fingers gripped her thighs to the point of almost being painful. "Mai, please," he managed to say between clenched teeth.

She tore open the package with her teeth and unwrapped the condom down his length. Vencel dropped his head back against the pillows, his body jerking under her. As soon as the condom completely sheathed him, he grabbed her hips and lifted her up. She could feel the wide tip pressing against her opening. "Fuck, Vencel, don't stop now."

His lips curled into an animalistic snarl, and he pulled her down on him, sheathing himself completely in one stroke. Mai felt as if she had been hit by lightning. The solid invasion of her body stretched her to the limit, but not pain. Still, it was almost enough to send her streaking toward a cliff she would happily jump off of into oblivion.

"Again." She tried to move, but Vencel held her in place.

"Not yet," he panted, "wait for Gaspar."

"You all right, *Angyalom*?" Gaspar whispered in her ear like a devil on her shoulder. "You still have room for me?"

Mai shuddered, a combination of nervousness and excitement. She wanted this more than anything. Being impaled by Vencel felt incredible, but something was missing. She needed this, needed to feel them both. "Please."

"Anything for you." He swirled a finger around her folds, making her body shake. He lifted his wet finger and wiped her own juices across her lips. "Now give Vencel a kiss."

"Oh, Christ, you're killing me here." Vencel pulled her down, and she eagerly pressed her lips against his. He licked at hers, moaning into her mouth. His tongue slid into her, and she sucked on it lightly, tasting her own essence.

She felt a cool gel on her bottom, as Gaspar rubbed at her back entrance. It felt deliciously sinful and taboo. She knew deep down that she never would have allowed anyone this kind of pleasure, except for these brothers. He pressed a thick finger against her, and she instinctively tightened up.

"You have to relax, *Angyalom*. Let me get you all slippery and I promise I won't hurt you."

Vencel cupped the back of her neck and pulled her down for another kiss while he slipped his hand between their bodies. His callused fingers found her delicate folds and stroked around the sensitive button hidden within. It was enough distraction that she relaxed, and Gaspar's finger slipped past her ring of muscles.

"Oh yea, that's it." He massaged the ring with more lube, and she felt the burning ease slightly. "One more finger, let me stretch you and get you ready."

The burning in her bottom eased, but the heat inside her rose with every stroke against her clit. Vencel nipped and licked at her lips, she met each stroke with one of her own. She moved her hips, trying to cause more friction on Vencel's cock. "More, dammit."

"You heard the lady, brother." Gaspar removed his fingers, and she felt them being replaced with something much larger. The blunt force pressing against her bottom had her trying to crawl up Vencel's body.

Gaspar gripped her hips, preventing her from going too far. Vencel slipped his cock to the very tip and then pushed back inside his full length. He flicked his thumb against her clit, and Mai saw stars. Another stroke and he pinched her clit between his fingers. Mai's senses went into overload, and she plunged into the flames they created inside her.

"That's it, *Nyuszikam*." Vencel pulled her down against his chest. "Push against that big cock."

She did as Vencel said and felt Gaspar slip past the strong ring of muscles. His cock stretched her to the limits, but there was no pain. Mai relaxed and felt Gaspar slip in deeper.

"Fuck, Mai. That's my girl, you can do it." He continued to press until she felt his body shudder. Gaspar slipped an arm around her ribs, holding her back against his chest. She blinked, feeling as if she has stars in her eyes. Her heart raced. She never felt this full in her entire life. "Now's the fun part."

Vencel's grin looked strained as he gripped her hips before sliding out. As he pressed back into her, Gaspar moved opposite, sliding out of her bottom. The feelings rippling through her felt dark and forbidden, making her want more. Moving in perfect tandem, the sensations amplified until Mai felt as though she floated in the middle of a vortex. Not knowing where one stopped and the other started. She grabbed on to Vencel's hand at her hip and on to the arm Gaspar wrapped around her, trying to stay grounded between the two of them. Their bodies were slick, and she easiy rocked between them as they drove into her, slamming her straight into another orgasm. This one coursed through her body like an inferno, taking over all her senses.

It felt as if they shared a body. She could hear the quiet night around their cabin and smell the forest. She knew where each animal hid and what they smelled like. She felt the exhilaration of running through the trees chasing prey. A primal, raw emotion slammed into her, tearing into her body and filling every cell to the brim like a massive dose of pain and pleasure all at once. A raw howl rang in her ears as if there were wolves in the room with them. Mai's scream joined them in a perfect blend of ecstasy. She collapsed on Vencel's chest, gasping for air and feeling as if her life would never be the same. His heart raced beneath her ear, and Gaspar lay over her back. She didn't feel the least bit crushed between them. It was more like feeling protected from the world.

Gaspar moved first, gently pulling out of her bottom making all three of them groan. She heard him pad out of the room and then water running in the bathroom. When he came back, Vencel moved her off him and to the side. She felt a warm cloth gently clean and pat her dry. Too exhausted to protest, she lay there and let them do what they wanted. The brother's muttered softly to each other, but she couldn't make out what they said. As soon as she got enough energy back, she would tell them whispering secrets was rude.

She never had the chance. Vencel slipped back into bed and pulled her against his side as Gaspar slid in behind her and laid over her like the best of heating blankets. She lasted ten seconds before falling fast asleep.

Chapter Eight

Mai woke to the incredible smell of fresh-roasted coffee. She crawled out of the large bed before she started to feel any more insecure. She had no idea what the proper protocol in this kind of situation was. Should she get her clothes and sneak out, or wander down the kitchen and get a coffee? For the first time in a long time, she decided to go ahead and do something and not worry so much about the consequences. If they didn't like her still being in their house, then she would leave. They didn't seem like complete assholes, so she didn't think they would order her out before she had a chance to drink a cup of coffee.

Funny how a simple decision could make her feel freer than she had in a long time. More confident even. She flopped back against the bed and pulled each pillow over her face and smelled them. It was weird, but she loved the way they smelled.

Vencel smelled like the forest. Almost like freshly dug earth and sandalwood with a bit of pine in the background, a free and wild smell. Different from Gaspar, who smelled like cedar and vanilla beans, more homey and comforting. Now if there was a cologne that combined all these scents, she would be a slave to whoever wore it.

She lay there and tried to amuse herself before finally giving up. Well, she wouldn't be going back to sleep now. She got up and padded over to the window, lifting the shade and opening the window. It was early. The sun had started to peak over the treetops, and she could smell the cool air from the forest. She loved it up here. Everything felt so much cleaner than in the city. The breeze felt fresh and full of oxygen, while in the city it hung hot and humid and felt like you were trying to breathe pea soup.

Now where the hell did my clothes go? Looking around the room, all she found was a large T-shirt lying at the end of the bed. Did they leave that for her? Okay, a bit strange, but she would have to go with it since she wasn't about to go downstairs naked.

She made her way down to the kitchen, where Gaspar looked up at her and sighed. "Dammit."

"What?" Mai gripped the banister and tried to put on a brave front, her insecurities whispering madly in her head. "What's the problem?"

"I bet Vencel twenty dollars you would ignore the T-shirt and come down here naked." He grinned up at her. "I hate losing to him, but I do like the look of you in that."

Mai glanced down at herself. The T-shirt that came halfway down her thighs, nothing embarrassing for him to see. *Go with it, Mai.* "Sorry to disappoint. Is that coffee I smell?"

"Ah, a woman after my own heart. Come on in. I just made a pot. How do you take yours?"

"Double double." She wandered over to the large, open sliding door to the deck. "You have a gorgeous home."

"Thanks. We've worked on it a lot lately." He handed her a steaming mug. Go ahead and explore if you like. I'm about to make breakfast."

"I usually only have coffee and a doughnut. I'm not a big eater." Her stomach chose that moment to announce its disagreement with that idea.

Gaspar grinned and caught her close to him, pressing a kiss to her neck. That subtle scent of cedar and vanilla beans washed over her, and Mai relaxed into his embrace. She imagined what it would be like to start every day like this, relaxed, calm, and cared for.

"Are you all right this morning?"

His words broke the spell his embrace had over her. She feared she had stepped over a line hugging him like this. She darted a quick look up at his face expecting to see evidence of his discomfort.

"We weren't too rough with you, were we?"

The concern in his eyes embarrassed her because she realized what he referred to. A silly thing, considering what they did the night before. His concern warmed her heart though. "I'm fine, really. I had a few sore muscles that haven't used in a long time."

"I'll get my brother to give you a massage. He's a master at them."

"Where is Vencel?" From what she noticed, the brothers weren't often apart. Must be a twin thing considering how close the two of them were.

"He'll be back in a little bit. We usually go out for a run in the morning before it gets too hot."

"You didn't want to today?"

"I didn't want you to wake up to an empty house and get it in your head we don't want you to be here."

"I don't want to wear out my welcome."

"That's not going to happen, Mai." He pressed a light kiss to her lips. "It's beautiful out on the deck. Go sit and relax, and I'll get breakfast ready."

"All right." Mai stepped out the sliding doors onto the deck. The wood felt damp under her feet and looked wet in the shade. It must have rained in the night, not that she would have noticed. She stepped out of the shadow of the house and into the sunshine. It was going to be a hot one today, the sun already felt warm on her legs. Their deck stretched out to two different levels. Perfect if you were the type to have a lot of parties. A hot tub sat on one of the platforms. Deep green vines grew on a trellis around it creating a natural shield. Not that anyone could see them here out in the middle of nowhere.

She propped her coffee on the railing and looked out over the clearing. Their house sat on the edge of a small lake, and she couldn't see any other buildings nearby. The lake looked black and dangerous. Mai hated water she couldn't see the bottom of. It always scared her. She'd watched one too many horror movies as a child.

The coffee was perfect, and the delicious aroma of bacon floated on the breeze. She opened her mouth to call out her compliments when something moved around the corner. At first she thought it was a dog. But it wasn't.

It was a very large fucking wolf. Mai froze for a moment, torn about what to do. Fear flooded her system, making her heart race and her legs shake. The wolf's hackles rose, and he growled low in his throat. Mai tried to work her throat, but the words lodged in there.

"*Do not run.*" Her brother's voice from a warning long ago echoed in her memories. Right, if she ran, the wolf would see her as prey and chase.

She stepped back away from the large animal. It stood there staring at her, but didn't move. She stepped another foot away. "Gaspar?" The words were no more than a whisper, but somehow he heard. Large arms wrapped around her from behind, trapping her against his chest.

"Vencel, you are the biggest asshole on the planet. We agreed this wasn't how we were going to tell her.

"Tell me what?" Mai looked around, but she couldn't see Vencel anywhere. She glanced back at Gaspar. "What the hell are we going to do?"

"*Nyuszikam,* I'm right here."

Mai slowly turned her head toward the wolf, only there wasn't a wolf there now. Only Vencel standing in the sun completely naked. While she appreciated the view, she managed to look away for a moment and search for the wolf. "What the hell? Where did the wolf go? Did you scare him off?"

She elbowed Gaspar in the stomach. "It's a pet, isn't it? You guys are complete jerks, scaring me like that."

"No, the wolf isn't a pet." Gaspar let go of her, and she walked away from him, reaching for her coffee.

"So what, you fed it a few times and now it's comfortable coming up on your deck? Do you know how dangerous that is?"

She took a sip of her coffee and looked back and forth to each of the brothers. There was something going on here, something creepy, and part of her felt like running fast and far.

"What?"

Vencel stepped closer to her and Mai instinctively stepped back, her fingers gripping the mug. "Okay, you two are freaking me out. What's the deal with the wolf?"

Gaspar sighed and then pulled off his T-shirt. "You had to push this didn't you?"

"It would have gotten harder to tell her, the longer we waited." Vencel shrugged one muscled shoulder. Following this conversation was almost impossible with Vencel's incredible body completely open to her perusal.

"Wait." She held up a hand, stopping Gaspar from slipping his already undone pants off his hips. "What are you two talking about?" *I love the little dip where his leg meets his hip.*

Gaspar smiled at her. "Mai, we have to tell you something really important."

"We aren't exactly what you think we are, *Nyuszikam.*"

"And what do you think you are?"

The air around Vencel's body shimmered as she watched. She blinked a couple times thinking her eyes were going out of focus, but her sight was fine everywhere else. Between one blink and the other Vencel disappeared and the wolf appeared again.

Mai's brain scrambled for a reasonable solution to what she saw. She turned to Gaspar who now stood as naked as Vencel had been. "You two are magicians?"

"No, Mai. Werewolves."

The same shimmering effect happened around Gaspar as if a layer of plastic wrap surrounded him and the sun reflected off it in all directions. Again, in a blink, the man disappeared, and in his place sat a large wolf, a twin to the wolf that Vencel had become.

Mai whipped her coffee cup at one wolf and took off running before she could form another thought. Her heart pounded hard in her chest, fear blinding her to anything but the need to survive. She headed for the open kitchen door and slammed it hard behind her. She heard a high-pitched yelp but didn't stop moving. Instead, she grabbed two large knives from the block in the kitchen and ran for the bathroom. Darting looks behind her, she was certain one of the wolves stood on his hind legs and looked up into the kitchen window. She didn't stop until she reached the bathroom. She quickly locked the door and backed away from it and into the tub. Her hands shook so badly, she placed the knives in the tub next to her.

Footsteps echoed on the stairs and into the room, stopping outside the door. "Mai, open the door."

"Fuck you!" Mai grabbed for the knives again holding them in front of her.

"Mai, I don't want you to hurt yourself. Unlock the door and I swear I will take you home right now. We didn't want to scare you, and I swear on my stupid brother's life that we won't harm you.

"Oh, I'm not going to hurt myself, but if either of you try to come in here, I'm going to go all Ginsu on your asses!"

"Okay, we won't, but would you come out here and talk?"

Mai could hear the hysteria in her own voice as she laughed at his suggestion. She had visions of the movie *The Shining*, only it would be a wolf's muzzle coming through the door and not Jack Nicholson. Well she wasn't going to lean on the wall and scream. Anyone who tried to come in here was going to be sorry.

"I think you might have broken Vencel's nose."

"Good!" Did she really feel bad about that? *Next thing I'll be opening the door and letting them have me for breakfast.* She couldn't have seen what she saw.

She could hear voices muttering low outside the door, tempting her to crawl over and try to eavesdrop. The idea that it might be a trap kept her still. Thankfully, she heard the footsteps walk away from the door. Her heart pounded like a freight train in her chest, and she couldn't stop her hands from shaking. Putting the knives down on the tub bottom next to her feet, she curled up and pulled her knees up to her chin.

She laid her cheek on her knees and tried to figure out what to do. Her cell was in the other room, so she couldn't call for help. *Breathe deep, you will figure this out.* For once, she didn't feel like she would freak out and cry....okay, she felt like she might cry, but she also wanted to run away. Could she escape from here?

Very slowly, she stood up and edged along the wall trying to see out with being seen. Part of her feared she would look over the edge and see one or both of them standing there.

Oh crap, can werewolves climb walls?

She reached over and engaged the locks, preventing the window from being opened. Then she took another deep breath and looked through the glass. No one was below, but it was too high up for her to try to jump. She might be able to do it, but risking a sprained ankle or broken leg wouldn't help her escape. *Don't panic. Think this through logically.*

This could all be a trick that backfired on them. Scaring the shit out of her and making her act like an ass. But then she couldn't change what she saw. Not once but twice. She stood where Gaspar stood moments before. There were no mirrors or strings or hidden floors. She heard footsteps again and hopped up on the counter so if they looked through the crack under the door they wouldn't be able to see her.

One of them knocked softly against the door, and she looked over at the tub where the knives lay. Stupid of her to let go of them, but who was she kidding? She'd more likely cut herself.

Another knock, this one a bit more forceful. "Mai? Are you all right?"

"You're joking right?" Thankfully, her tone sounded stronger than she felt.

"Don't do anything stupid in there, okay." She could hear more muttering and a thud. Sounded like someone punched another person. Being closer to the door this time, she could hear Gaspar snarling. She didn't know how she could tell them apart without seeing them, but deep down she knew the difference between the two out there.

"Vencel, how's your nose?" *I'm an idiot.*

"Sore."

"Nothing he didn't deserve," Gaspar added before grunting as if he took a hit to the stomach. That sound she recognized since her own brothers were never above giving each other a shot now and again.

"Mai, I'm really sorry for scaring you like this. I thought that telling you bluntly would be the best way to go. You know, like taking off a bandage."

"I'll remember that the next time I get cut."

"Mai, did you cut yourself?" Gaspar's voice sounded panicked. "I didn't smell any blood."

"No, I'm not hopeless, and the only one getting cut will be the first person to open that door."

"We're not going to try, promise."

They didn't sound like they stood close to the door, so Mai took a chance and quietly slipped to the floor. Tiptoeing to the bathtub she lifted each knife out and placed them on the counter before sitting on the tub's edge. She was hiding in a bathroom with nothing but two knives and a small lock on the door. On the other side of the door were two shape-shifters that she had sex with many times last night. She moaned and dropped her head into her hands.

"Mai, are you hungry?"

"Go away!" She waited, listening, but didn't hear a thing. *Did they leave?* Taking a peek was a temptation she had to resist. *Because if you don't, then what?*

As much as she wanted to ignore that little voice in her head, it had a point. If the boys wanted to hurt her, then she doubted a simple lock wouldn't have stopped them. In fact, she could have been killed a dozen times over in the last few hours if they really wanted to. The entire idea seemed so extreme, so fantastic, it couldn't be true. How many old villagers told her stories as she grew up? Stories about local legends and supernatural beings. She remembered reading that every legend starts from a fact or grain of truth. *Could werewolves be real?*

She sat there staring out the window, for about an hour she figured, going over everything that happened in her mind. The way they took care of her. Gaspar holding her when she felt as though she would fall apart because she felt so scared. Vencel looking so incredibly ashamed of his actions in the restaurant. They hadn't given her any reason to think they would hurt her, more the opposite. This is what they must mean by being trapped between a rock and a hard place. She sat at a crossroads, and there weren't any other options open to her. *So now what?*

"Are you still out there?" It felt silly to say it out loud, but she needed to know.

"Yes." They answered in stereo, but they didn't sound close to the door.

"You're not going to go away, are you?"

"Mai, we can't."

They must be afraid that she would run to a grocery store checkout rag or to the newspapers or RCMP. "I won't tell anyone. I'll keep your secret."

She recognized Vencel's laugh at her words. "*Nyuszikam*, we aren't worried about that. We want to make certain that you are all right in there. While hiding in a bathroom has certain conveniences, I'm not sure how long you would last in there."

Okay, even she had to admit that this situation was getting silly. Part of her brain already started to rationalize the entire event. Maybe she didn't see what she thought, even if it happened a few feet away from her in broad daylight. She picked up the knives and slowly tiptoed to the door. "If I come out, you two have to stay away from me."

"Vencel and I will stay right where we are."

Mai opened the door open a crack and peered out. Both men were on the other side of the room. Vencel stood with his arms crossed over his chest, and Gaspar sat on the end of the bed. She opened the door a bit more and stepped into the room. Her hands clenched the handle of the knives. Slipping along the wall she moved slowly to the door.

"*Angylom*, what did we do to make you not trust us?" Gaspar looked as if someone had kicked his puppy.

"Turned into a fucking wolf." She looked at Vencel. "And you growled at me!"

He had the decency to look sheepish. "It wasn't at you. I could smell your fear, and it made me angry. I never want you to be frightened of us."

"Sometimes our reactions in wolf form don't translate well," Gaspar added. "We'll do everything we can to keep you safe."

"So the wolf thing…" Mai didn't really know what to ask. She had a hundred ideas going through her head and a thousand questions.

"Why don't you put the knives down for now." Vencel spoke softly, his words almost soothing.

Mai glanced at the large weapons. He had a point. Standing here holding them was starting to make her feel stupid. She placed the knives on the dresser next to the door and immediately felt two large arms wrap around her torso.

"Now, you're ours."

She wriggled in Gaspar's embrace. "Put me down, you animal. You said you would stay right where you were."

He didn't and instead carried her over to the bed where Vencel now waited. He sat in the middle of it, and when Gaspar tossed her down, he grabbed her wrists and pinned them to the bed over her head.

"And we will. Only I thought it would be better if you were over here with us."

"What are you doing?" She could feel the T-shirt had ridden up her legs, and at the moment she wasn't certain it covered anything.

"Keeping you here in one spot while we talk. I want to make certain that you don't try to run off again."

Gaspar stretched our along her side. "Ask."

"Ask what?"

"Anything you want, you ask and we'll answer."

"So why is Vencel holding me like this?"

"Because we plan to amuse ourselves as you shoot out your questions."

That sounded incredible, and Mai's traitorous body responded as she always did when she was near them. She could feel her body arching up into the hand that he lay just under her breasts.

"So obviously you can change anytime you want?"

"Yes." Gaspar nuzzled the skin behind her knee. He lifted her leg up so much, she was certain that he could see every inch of her. "The whole full moon bit is an exaggeration. Shifting at a full moon is more tradition than necessity.

"Next question?" Vencel brought one hand to his lips and pressed his lips to the back of it.

"Can silver bullets kill you?"

"You still planning our demise, huh?"

"You scared the shit out of me, so yes I may keep a mental plan for a while."

Vencel chuckled against her elbow before licking it. What she thought would be weird actually turned her on. Who knew her inner elbow would prove to be so sensitive?

"We can be killed by bullets, but they don't have to be made of silver." Gaspar looked incredibly serious. "We heal quicker than humans, so a flesh wound won't slow us down as much, but if we are hit in a vital organ, then we would die."

"And if you bit me?"

"You would cream yourself…more." Gaspar nipped at her earlobe, and indeed her body heated up, and she could feel herself growing more slippery by the moment.

"If you broke the skin when you bit me, would I turn furry at the next full moon?"

Vencel's laugh vibrated against her neck. "We aren't controlled by moon cycles, remember?"

"Oh yeah, I forgot."

Gaspar tilted her face in his direction, while Vencel pressed kisses against her shoulder. "Being a shape-shifter isn't a disease or curse. It's what we are, so to answer your question, no, you would never be able to turn into a wolf."

"Oh, well, that's a relief. No offense, but I have enough to deal with myself. I don't think I could handle something else."

"Are there a lot of your race?"

"Sadly no. Many have been hunted to extinction. If we die in wolf form, we stay in that form unlike what you see in the movies. Children are a rare blessing, so our numbers don't increase quickly."

"Does that mean you belong to a pack?"

"There is a pack up here in the park, and we do answer to the Alpha out of respect. He knows we don't have any interest in pack politics and won't come after his position."

"Did you ever belong to a pack?"

"Yes, in Hungary. The lupine packs are very structured there."

She turned to Vencel. "Is that the language you were speaking to the sausage vendor outside the Toronto Star building?"

"How do you know it was me?"

"I'm not sure, but I know it wasn't Gaspar. Isn't that a bit strange?"

"Not at all." Gaspar pressed a kiss above her belly button. "Do you have any more questions?"

"Why did you leave Hungary?"

"Because we were being hunted during the war and thought it would be safer for everyone if we didn't stay around."

Mai could hear the pain echoing behind Vencel's words. Obviously they didn't want to leave. She curled her finger at him and he bent closer. "What is it?"

Mai kissed him on the tip of his nose. "I'm sorry I slammed the door on you."

"It's all right, *Nyuszikam*. I promise you it doesn't hurt anymore." He pressed a soft kiss on her temple. "I'm sorry I frightened you so much."

Gaspar pressed a kiss to her hip. "We want you to stay here, Mai. Stay with us."

Mai sat up, not certain why they were so focused on her. "I can't just leave my home and everything. I hardly know either of you."

"And that is exactly what we want to rectify." He laid a hand over her knee. "Stay a few more days, *Angyalom*. I promise no more secrets."

"Okay, but I want to call Stephanie. She gets nervous if she doesn't hear from me."

"Mai, you understand that sense of smell is elevated, right?"

"How elevated?"

"We can smell your creamy pussy from here," Gaspar pressed a kiss against her hipbone. Vencel nuzzled her neck. "And we know you lied about having to call Stephanie. But do it anyways because we want you to be comfortable."

"I didn't…" Both men looked at her as if they dared her to lie. "You're not going to stand over me when I talk?"

"Not at all. In fact, why don't you take the phone out onto the deck, and I'll start breakfast again." Mai refused to feel guilty over breakfast being delayed, but now that Gaspar mentioned it, she realized she was starving. "All right, but I can only stay a day or two. I have to work."

Vencel gently bit the side of her neck. "That smells like a half lie I think, but I'll let you get away with it for now." He crawled off the bed and held his hand out to Mai. "Come on, *Nyuszikam*, I don't know about you, but I'm starving."

Mai crawled to the edge of the bed and took Vencel's hand. Part of her was annoyed that they didn't continue what they started, but then considering what happened, she should have expected it. Nothing like having a woman hide in the bathroom with knives to put a damper on any feelings.

Gaspar grinned at her as he gracefully moved off the bed in front of them.

"What's so funny?"

"You are, and I like that." Gaspar cupped her cheeks with his hands and brushed a light kiss against her lips. Mai's eyes fluttered closed as soon as she realized his intent. The man could kiss like a dream.

"I could watch the two of you all day. Damn, this feels good."

Mai wasn't certain how to take that but filed the question away for the time being. Right now she really needed to talk to her best friend.

Chapter Nine

"Oh my goodness, Mai, I've been so worried." Her best friend almost sounded frantic on the other line. "It's been days since I heard from you."

"I'm sorry, Steph. I've had a few shocks in my life over the past couple days. How are Mabelle and Brodie?"

"They're fine. What do you mean shocks?"

Mai thought it a bit strange that Steph would brush off talking about her family so quickly. Usually Mai could count on at least a ten-minute marathon from Steph regarding the wonders of her baby and husband.

"Have you talked to your family recently?"

"No, why?

"Your brother phoned here the other day looking for you. He said that he couldn't get a hold of you."

"Crap, I forgot to tell them I lost my phone. Did you tell him?"

"Yuppers, I did, and I told him you were on a women's retreat and would be back in a week."

"Why did you tell him that?"

"Because he seemed anxious to talk to you, and I figured you wouldn't want him crashing your party."

Mai leaned against the deck railing and looked over the yard to the wooded area to the side of the house. She wanted to tell Steph so much but knew she couldn't, and that fact hurt.

"Mai, you there?"

"Yes, sorry, I was thinking."

"So what do you think about the Solfalvi brothers?"

"They are amazing, and wow, I don't think I can put it in words."

"I remember feeling the same way about Brodie. He took my breath away, and it scared the shi...dickens out of me."

Hearing her friend's continuing effort to temper her language made her smile.

"Brodie told me that twin shape-shifters are incredibly rare."

Mai felt as if the world tilted sharply to the left, or more accurately she suddenly found herself in a Douglas Adams book. Lifting the phone away from her ear, she looked to make certain she dialed the correct number. "Um Steph, do you have Rod Sterling standing next to you?"

"Oh, that guy from the old *Twilight Zone* TV show, right? Brodie and I have almost all the seasons on DVD."

"Steph," Mai snapped, "why are you talking about shape-shifters like this? What, do you believe they exist?"

A pregnant silence stilled the phone line.

"Well, remember when I said I met Brodie on a camping trip with my family?"

"Yes!" Mai thought for a moment that perhaps she really had somehow stepped into the twilight zone because this couldn't all be real.

"Well, Brodie used to work as a handyman up in the area of my parents' cottage.

"Yeah, they have the place up on Georgian Bay. I've been there with you."

"Brodie lived up there for a very long time and helped out the locals. He heard a lot while he pretended to raid the garbage dump."

"Oh my god, Steph." Mai felt her knees getting weak and she sank down onto the wooden deck. Sitting under the hot sun, she tried to make sense of it all.

"What about baby Belle?"

"Brodie said it's a good possibility that she will be able to shape-shift as well. There isn't a guarantee, but because pregnancies are so rare, the animal gene tends to be dominant."

"Doesn't that freak you out?"

"No, not really, but then I've had time to get used to it."

"Well, then what pack does Brodie belong to?"

"He doesn't belong to a pack, Mai. Brodie is a bear. Are you okay, Mai? You're not going to freak out, right? Brodie told me not to say anything to you yet, but I hate keeping secrets from you. I've kept this one for two years, and I hated not telling you. I'm so relieved to be able to talk mate to mate…"

"Mate? You used that term the other day. What does it mean?"

"All I can tell you is how it works with bears, although Brodie says that all shape-shifters are similar. They can have sex with whoever they want and bond with one person and form a lasting relationship, just like us. It's all about free choice and apparently Mother Nature doesn't like to mess with that too much.

A man can bond with almost anyone, but sooner or later they will feel the divide of their species and need to move on. But there is something very special called a True Mate. It's more than simply magic. They really do have soul mates, and when True Mates bond, they're together forever."

After she finished talking to Steph, Mai sat out on the deck under the sunshine until Vencel came out for her.

"I think you have had enough shocks today, *Nyuszikam*, especially on an empty stomach."

"My best friend is married to a bear…" Mai felt as if someone came along and ripped the rug right out from under her feet.

"Yes, I know. Your friend gave him Gaspar's number the night of that terrible first date. He phoned and threatened to disembowel both of us if we didn't fix everything immediately.

"So everything you said is because of Brodie?"

"Fuck no. I don't give a shit about that grumpy bear. He couldn't have made us do anything we didn't want to do. Mai, we brought you up here because we thought you were special, and we wanted to get to know you better."

"No ulterior motives?"

"We're wolves, and one bear doesn't scare us." He lifted her up into his arms. "Come on. You need something to eat."

As soon as he swept her off her feet, Mai felt every muscle in her body relax. Resting her head on his shoulder this way, she could smell that forest and sandalwood scent that was so unique to him. Learning Brodie and Steph's secret sent her thoughts spinning, but feeling the strength of Vencel's arms holding her up helped combat the anxiety that should be overwhelming her by now. Instead, she felt safe and secure.

Vencel carried her into the kitchen where the incredible smell of bacon came back as well as maple syrup. Her stomach growled low and long. She tried to curl into herself to hide it, but both men couldn't help but laugh, and Mai joined them.

Gaspar placed a large plate of pancakes and bacon in front of her. "Oh my god, I didn't realize how hungry I was until I smelled this." She cut the pancakes with a fork and ate a large dripping piece. She moaned as she chewed. "This is so good."

"*Angyalom,* if you promise to make those noises again, I'll cook you whatever you want." Gaspar sat next to her and began eating his way through a larger stack of pancakes.

Vencel got up and refilled their juice and everyone's coffee cups.

They sat there and ate in companionable silence for a bit. Mai ate more than she had in her entire life. Everything tasted so incredible. "Gaspar you are an amazing cook. I think I might explode." She picked up her plate, but Gaspar took it out of her fingers.

"I'm glad you like it, and we are both thrilled you have such a good appetite." He took the plate and stepped away to add it to the dishwasher.

Vencel reached out and snaked his arm around her waist, pulling her back closer to him and into his lap. Mai felt a little awkward, but he seemed much happier to have her here. After a few moments, she relaxed and leaned slightly against him, resting her head on his shoulder again. This was more comfortable than she could ever imagine.

"We were a bit concerned when we went out to dinner and you only ate a salad. Gaspar said you wanted to go to that place." Vencel relaxed back in his seat, a coffee in his one hand. His other rested against her waist. His thumb idly stroked the bottom of her ribs.

Gaspar sat down next to them and reached out for her hand. He lightly stroked her hands while she spoke.

"When I get nervous, I get nauseous, and then I get panicky and feel like I'm going to throw up, so I tend to pick at my food. That way I can make sure nothing embarrassing happens."

Gaspar gave her a questioning look. "You suffer from panic attacks? *Angyalom*, you hide them very well."

How could she explain the need to hide her weakness when she didn't understand it herself? "But what is really strange is that it doesn't happen when I'm with either of you."

"Of course not." Vencel's tone sounded a tad arrogant. Mai sat up and looked at him. "You're ours, and you trust us."

"I think that's a pretty quick assumption since really I hardly know either of you." Mai wanted to believe him, but what would stop them from leaving her?

Vencel smacked his coffee cup on the table, making her jump. Spearing his fingers through her hair, he pulled her face close to his. He looked so pissed off but still handled her gently. "*Nyuszikam*, you know our biggest secret, and one day you will read us as well as we read you. Don't ever doubt that.'

"I don't understand."

Vencel let go of her hair, and Gaspar caught her chin, turning her head toward him. He braced one hand on the table and held onto her chin with the other. "You are our True Mate, Mai Bennett. Ours forever, and the bond we are forming now will only grow stronger over time. You have mated with twin wolves, which put you in a unique situation. Vencel and I can sense each other's thoughts and in time, you will as well."

"You mean I will read your minds?"

"In a way, yes. You will sense what we are thinking, and the bond will translate it into words. It will always be there regardless of whether we are in wolf or human form."

"Wow, that's kind of scary."

Vencel laughed against her neck, and Gaspar pressed a kiss to her forehead. "You'll get used to it." He leaned back a bit. "What would you like to do today?"

Mai remembered that afternoon in the park the day she met Gaspar. At the time, he mentioned something she wanted to experience but wasn't certain how to ask."

"Laying in the sunshine, *Angyalom*?"

"You said you wouldn't be able to read my mind for a while."

"No, he said you wouldn't be able to. We can already figure out what you are thinking to a certain extent."

"That doesn't seem fair."

"I think it is. Gaspar and I will always tell you what we want and not be embarrassed about it in the least. If you're not certain how to ask something, we can figure out what you want and need."

"Oh, well, if you put it that way..." An illicit thought ran though Mai's mind, and she wondered if he would pick up on it.

He did because in a blur of movement she found herself sitting on the edge of the table. Gaspar pulled her T-shirt off her upraised arms, and Vencel buried his face between her breasts. "Wait, this isn't what I was thinking," she managed to get out between gasps of breath.

"It's not an exact science." Gaspar cupped her cheek and nipped at her lower lip. "Whatever you thought turned you on enough to flood that beautiful pussy of yours with cream."

"We need strawberries." Vencel licked the underside of her breasts, making her feel like the air conditioning had turned off. She ran her fingers along his hairline and through the silky mass over one of his ears. With the other hand, she reached out and pressed the heel of her palm against the straining muscle behind Gaspar's zipper. He growled low in his throat and attacked her, kissing her as if he meant to devour her. She couldn't get enough. The world seemed to tilt for her as Gaspar encouraged her to lie back on the table. Vencel lifted her hips, and she felt her shorts and panties slip down her legs.

Gaspar's hand lay over her breasts, and a possessive feeling rushed through her, as did an electrical tingle from Vencel's lips against her inner thigh. She wriggled in his hold, waiting for him to move the last inch and lick her core, but it never happened. Her body thrummed with anticipation, but both men froze. Concern battered at Mai's self-confidence as both Gaspar and Vencel moved quickly away from her. *Did I do something wrong or miss a clue?*

"*Nyuszikam,* quickly, take this." He pressed her clothes into her hands. "Run upstairs quickly and get dressed."

"But I…"

"*Angyalom,* there is someone coming up the drive."

"Fuck, they're wolves." Vencel took her by the hand and scooped her up into his arms. Running upstairs to the bathroom, he placed her in the tub and handed her a gun.

"Holy shit, Vencel. I don't know how to use that!"

"Give me your hand."

"No, I don't want it. Vencel, you're scaring me."

He leaned forward and wrapped his arms around her, his unique scent surrounding her. She felt the icy anxiety clawing at her dissipate leaving behind a sense of calm. "*Nyuszikam,* don't be frightened. You'll be fine. We're not expecting trouble, but we aren't willing to take any chances with you." He put the weapon in her hand and her finger on the trigger. "See this switch, it's the safety, and it's on. If you hear someone walking toward the door, flick off the safety. Press here, see the red light?"

Mai nodded her head. Her heart pounded wildly against her chest

"Aim it at the door. If the door opens, start shooting. Where the light hits is where the bullet will go."

"But what if it's you?"

"We will call out first. Don't worry." He pressed a kiss against her forehead. Whatever you do, keep it pointed away from you, all right? I promise I'll train you on the proper use soon, but today you are getting the down and dirty instructions."

"How do you know these are bad wolves?"

"We don't, but we aren't taking any chances with you."

The sound of car doors slamming sounded like a death knell outside. Mai felt like she wanted to throw up. "Are you going to be okay?"

"I swear to you Gaspar and I will be fine. This is simply a precaution. Be as quiet as possible, and we will come back for you in a few minutes."

Vencel moved to the doorway. "Lock the door behind me, Mai."

She nodded, and as soon as the door closed, she pushed the little button in. The gun felt much heavier than she expected, and she hated the feel of it in her hand. Holding it away from her and pointing it away, she backed up to the opposite corner and slid down the wall. Placing the gun on the floor next to her, she rubbed her damp palms on her legs. What the hell did she get herself in the middle of?

Chapter Ten

Gaspar stood out on the porch of their home and crossed his arms over his chest. Gordon, the local pack alpha, knew better than to arrive unannounced. He would have called first. Anyone from town and he would have recognized their scents on the breeze. Gaspar couldn't help the sense of relief that the wind blew in the direction it did. It gave him and Vencel an opportunity to hide Mai. They were out of practice of being so careful.

That is how you lost a mate, by assuming there wasn't someone skulking in the shadows waiting to take them away from you. That's the lesson he and Vencel learned before they left their home country. He saw a number of their pack lose a mate and then die from loneliness within a short period of time. Most of them ventured out in a mad killing spree until they were either killed or died themselves. Now, having a mate tucked away upstairs, Gaspar could understand completely why despair and grief could drive a mate mad. If anything happened to Mai, he could easily see himself stepping back and letting his primal self loose.

A pristine black Mercedes crept up the narrow driveway to his home, and the scent of wolf hit him harder. They weren't from the local pack. This scent hadn't touched his senses in sixty-five years. His wolf clawed at him, demanding to be released, to punish those that dared to enter his territory uninvited. Gaspar allowed his hands to shift. His fingers snapped and elongated, the skin splitting and reforming around deadly claws. The pain was a welcome feeling, sending a burst of adrenaline through his system. It took a moment to regain enough control to stop it there. He wanted to shift more but knew that might hinder him.

The car stopped far from the house and the driver's and passenger's doors opened simultaneously. Tall, bulky men got out of the car and looked around before focusing on Gaspar. They might think they have the odds in their favor, but that would be foolish on their parts. One large advantage of twins is that they fought like a team. He and Vencel could link their thoughts and fight as an extension of each other, a definite advantage in this situation. He allowed a loud rolling growl to rumble from between his lips as he stepped down the stairs to the gravel drive. He wanted this intruder to know he wasn't welcome in their home. One of the shifters walked to the back door and opened it, allowing an older man to emerge from the back.

Neither he nor Vencel moved to greet or welcome this elder. Timur Denescz encouraged them to flee their homeland, and then he took over as leader. Gaspar never liked him, but at the time, he and Vencel had no choice since their pack mates were dying at alarming rates all in defense of him and his brother. Vencel stepped up beside him and snarled as soon as he recognized their old advisor.

Mai?

Bathroom again. She ran there earlier, so I figured that she would feel safer in there. I left the gun with her, too. Hopefully, she won't have to use it.

Gaspar nodded slightly. Poor Mai, if this didn't send her running terrified from them, then they might have a chance. Although, the idea of her running and the two of them hunting her made his wolf hungry.

"Gaspar, Vencel! Please excuse my unannounced visit." Timur strutted up the drive toward them.

"Your guard dogs stay at the car." Gaspar pointed a clawed finger at the two bodyguards. They both looked at their boss before accepting his nod.

"I'm shocked you would receive a pack mate in such a manner. Living here in Canada has destroyed your manners. I should have insisted you both return years ago."

"You really think we would listen to you?" Vencel stepped forward, his voice deceptively calm. Vencel had the ability to keep himself completely under control and then shift at a moment's notice and tear a swath through whatever threatened him.

"Of course, dear boy." Despite their answering in English, Timur continued to speak in Hungarian, which annoyed Gaspar even more. The lack of respect this old one used was typical of his generation and upbringing.

"You are of the Bükk pack. I encouraged you to cross to this country to help saves your lives. The time has come for you to return home."

"We are home. This is our place, and it's where we will stay."

Timur looked around a slightly distasteful look on his face. "I can see the attraction to this part of the country, but their cities are sterile and lacking any kind of culture or history. Our home has an ancestry rich with memories."

"And by staying here we will make our own memories." The afternoon breeze shifted, and Gaspar knew that Timur picked up what they were trying to hide.

"Really boys, if I interrupted something, you really should have said so." He shook his head at them as if disappointed. Knowing the strict rules of their old pack, the elder probably viewed them as wild teenagers pushing acceptable boundaries. "I'll let you boys get back to your fun. Next time please tell me before I make a special trip out here. A simple voice message would have sufficed."

Vencel stalked forward, but Gaspar grabbed his arm. As much as he would have loved to tear into the interlopers, neither did he want a full force descending on him. Timur wasn't stupid. He wouldn't have shown up without a backup situated somewhere close.

"I am staying at the poor excuse for a hotel in Ecstasy Lake. It's the best place I could find in the area, but since we are only staying a few days to help you clear up any matters here, I figured we could rough it." He sniffed the air again and smiled at them. "I'll see the two of you at my hotel this afternoon, and bring your human. I'd like to meet her."

Vencel growled at them, and Gaspar tightened his hold on his brother's arm. "We'll see you then."

Timur got back into his car while his lapdogs continued to scan the area. What did they think was going on here? Obviously, Vencel and Gaspar were the only shape-shifters in the immediate area, but they needed to look useful or the old man would get rid of them, too.

The cars backed away, but neither he nor Vencel acknowledged the retreating wave. Both of them stood there with their arms crossed. Gaspar's wolf wasn't ready to recede yet, so he didn't fight it. They both stood there until the foreign wolves' scent trailed away.

"We aren't taking her."

"We have to, or they will call a hunt on her. Denescz isn't as stupid as I wish. He will know that she is special to us. Her scent must have mingled with ours by now."

"I don't like this."

"Neither do I"

Gaspar felt his wolf straining to break loose. He wanted blood and revenge on those who would come to his den and threaten the safety of his family.

"Why don't you take a run in the forest? You're so agitated that Mai might not believe you when you try to tell her that everything is okay."

"But it's not okay."

"She doesn't need to know that right now."

* * * *

"Mai it's me." Vencel called out as soon as he walked back into the house. "Everything is all right. I'm coming up the stairs, put the gun down now."

He could hear her moving in the bathroom but didn't hear the sound of the gun being laid down. Concern struck his heart, and he raced up the stairs two at a time. *"Nyuszikam,* are you all right?"

"Yes." The lock on the bathroom door clicked, and she poked her head around the crack. When she saw Vencel, she breathed a long sigh of relief. He heard the slight clunk when she placed the gun on the tiled counter. Part of him wanted to congratulate her for thinking of her safety first, but it was overruled by the need to comfort her. He opened his arms, and she ran into them. Jumping into his arms, she wrapped her arms around his neck and her legs around his waist.

"I was so scared, and I'm not certain why."

He kissed her for being so very brave. She must have been picking up on his and Gaspar's concern. *Could their bond be that strong already?* "I told you there was nothing to worry about."

"Where is Gaspar?"

"He's out running and trying to work off some of his aggravation. His wolf prowled too close to the surface, and he didn't want to frighten you any more than you already were."

"That's thoughtful, but really if we are going to be together for a while, then you guys need to let me see all aspects of you. Not only the parts you are willing to show me…"

"I'll remember that." He walked over to the bed and lay her down on it. Those assholes had ruined his morning snack, and he decided to make up for it. Mai flopped back on the bed with a smile.

"Looks like I need to unwrap you again."

"Does that make me your present?"

"Absolutely, and it feels like my birthday every day." He smiled down at her, proud of the way she kept herself together. He expected her to be a crying mess by the time he came back up here, but his Mai showed him a glimpse of her ironclad soul. That she would beat these panic attacks she suffered from he had no doubt. Mai didn't know it, but he admired her strength. "Can you tell what I'm thinking right now?"

"No, should I?"

"Close your eyes." He watched as she did as he asked and then peeled her T-shirt off her. Her eyes opened, and he could see the humor in her depths. "Close them, cheater."

Her laugh sent a bolt of pure sunshine into his heart. Now he understood why Gaspar wanted so desperately to find their mate. If he knew this is what it would be like, he would have hunted alongside him much sooner than this.

"I want you to relax." He trailed his fingers along her collar bone and down between her breasts. "Think about the way you feel for us. Let that feeling fill you."

Affection and something stronger batted at his senses. They were Mai's emotions, and for her to care so much already made Vencel want to fall to his knees and worship her. Whether she realized it or not her emotions were already engaged with his brother and himself. He unbuttoned her shorts and slid both them and her panties off her. He planned to destroy every pair of underwear she owned. That way he would only be one layer of clothing between her and his hands.

"Now what are you feeling, *Nyuszikam*. You can brush aside your feelings for us, what is left?"

"I don't think…it's like you are, I don't know, I can't say…"

"It's not easy to put feeling into words is it?" He gently pressed her legs, and they fell apart. She concentrated so hard on trying to read him, she wasn't paying attention to what he did to her. He nuzzled her thighs and kissed a path up the inside of each leg to her core.

"What are you feeling, Mai? Where's Gaspar?"

"Running…" She sighed and moved restlessly against his hands. "He is angry and wants…he's afraid of hurting…of hurting me?"

"Very good, *Nyuszikam*" He trailed up the other leg and paused above her dampened curls. "What about me, Mai."

"I don't know…"

"Yes, you do. Say it." He licked lightly up one fold, her taste exploded on his tongue. If filled his senses, he wanted more but not yet…he reined in his hunger sharply.

"Are you proud of me?"

"That's right." He pressed a couple fingers against her delicate skin, pressing them apart exposing the hard nubbin hiding within.

"Oh, Vencel, please."

"You know what I want, *Nyuszikam*"

It's not possible…too soon."

"No, *Nyuszikam*. It's never too soon." He knew that he loved her already. He wanted to destroy anything that made her frightened, and that meant he would get to the bottom of whatever caused these panic attacks. He sucked her clit into his mouth and flicked it with his tongue. Mai dug her heels into the bedding and almost completely lifted herself off the bed.

"Oh god, yes…"

He continued to flick at her clit with his tongue, feeling his cock press hard against his jeans. Mai wreathed under his mouth, and when he slid a couple fingers inside her, she screamed out his name. Moisture flooded his fingers and mouth, and he licked up her delicious cream as quickly as he could. She continued to shiver under him.

He mentally offered thanks to his brother for the foresight to litter the house with condoms as soon as they brought Mai here. He grabbed one out of the nightstand and quickly sheathed himself. Pressing within her welcoming heat, he felt her body squeeze him in a rhythm all her own. Mai gripped his hair and pulled his mouth against hers.

Knowing she tasted herself on his lips drove him over the edge, and he pistoned himself within her. Pulling her legs up over his shoulders, he angled his hips, stroking deeper to reach that perfect spot within her. As soon as he stroked it, he knew. Her eyes opened wide as he continued to pump against the same spot repeatedly.

"Vencel. I can't...

"Yes, you can, *Nyuszikam*. One more just for me..." Reaching between her legs, he slipped his fingers between her swollen dripping folds to stroke the sensitive little nubbin protected within.

She gripped his arms, her small nails breaking the skin, as she strained against him. The most incredibly beautiful look crossed over her face before she hollered out his name loud enough to make his ears ring. Heat washed over his cock as her body squeezed him and then fluttered along his length pulling him over the edge with her.

Chapter Eleven

"You plan to give up your birthright then?"

Timur Denescz was the creepiest looking old man Mai had ever met, regardless of the expensive suit he wore. Had she seen him before, she would never have agreed to come here today. The boys told her about his request to meet her, but so far, he hadn't even looked at her. According to them, this meeting was out of respect for their old pack, but they wouldn't stay long.

"What birthright?" Mai looked up at Gaspar and then Vencel. Both her men glared at the man pacing in front of them.

Timur turned his head and glanced at her. A mix of surprise and disgust colored his features, as if he couldn't believe that she dared speak in his presence.

"Their inherent place within the strongest pack in Europe, of course. The gift of offspring is rare enough for our people, and a multiple birth is almost unheard of." Timor's eye narrowed on her, and she felt true fear hit her directly in the heart. "I refuse to allow the two of you to throw that away for nothing but a pathetic, weak biped."

A harsh, animalistic growl filled the air, not that Mai saw anything because Gaspar moved in front of her. Reaching back he hugged her to his back with one hand. He then stepped back, forcing her to move with him and angled them until he had her backed into a corner. She gripped handfuls of his shirt and stayed put. She saw lots of movies where the woman tried to be brave, but she wasn't stupid. If he wanted her out of sight, then she would stay right there.

"You," the word didn't sound like it came from Vencel, but she knew it did, even with the animalistic sound to his voice, "don't ever look at our woman like that again."

"Didn't...mean..." Timur's voice sounded thin and reedy as he gasped for air between each word.

A steady, low growl vibrated in Gaspar's chest and every muscle in his body stayed tense. She pressed her face against his back, and despite the severity of the situation, she felt his hand stroke her lower back. They were in the middle of a huge clusterfuck that apparently she caused by speaking, and he was trying to comfort her? Could she give them up if she had to?

Gaspar snarled and squeezed her tightly, as if he heard her thought. Of course according to Vencel, they could to a certain extent.

"If anyone touches a hair on our woman's head," Gaspar's voice sounded deeper than normal as well, and it vibrated unnaturally, "we will hunt you and your men down and shred you with our bare claws."

"Our place is here, in our home with our woman." Vencel must have gotten himself back under control because his voice sounded more human again. Mai shifted her weight and peeked around Gaspar's arm. The older man stood hunched over, his hand gripping the back of a nearby chair. His other hand rubbed his own neck.

"That pack structure here is completely disorganized. They have no recognized hierarchy. You are royalty. You have a duty to seed the pack."

"So that is why you want us so bad." Gaspar shook his head in disgust. "You have inbred yourselves to the point of destruction and infertility.

"You have no business thinking of bonding with a biped. Dirty humans almost cost us our pack."

"The elders' refusal to respect the humans' power is what almost destroyed the pack. You figured as long as you kept to the mountains they wouldn't bother you. Instead, we were hunted to near extinction."

There was a soft knock at the door before it opened. A woman walked through, shorter than Mai but gorgeous. Long, golden blonde hair flowed over her shoulders, pinned up on one side with a large gerbera daisy. "Oh, Papa, I'm sorry, I thought you were alone."

Yeah whatever. Mai didn't believe her for a second, and if this is what the women looked like in Hungary, then she expected to be left in the dust.

"It's fine. Gentlemen, this is my daughter, Marika. I had hoped that you would find her a suitable candidate for the position we spoke of."

The woman looked over both men with an appreciative smile on her face.

Oh, I don't think so. Mai slipped around Gaspar's large frame and stood in front of him. Crossing her arms, she gave this Marika her best "fuck off and die" glare. Marika gave her a curious frown when she glanced over at her.

Gaspar's arms wrapped around Mai's shoulders, and she felt him rest his chin on the top of her head. She could feel the tension radiating off his body, and a growl seemed to continuously rumble in his chest. She rubbed the forearms wrapped protectively around her in hopes of calming him down some. Whatever was going on, she didn't want to be a part of it and getting out of here felt like a top priority.

"What position are you looking for gentlemen? I'll help with what I can."

Could it be possible that this woman didn't know what her father planned? The way her gaze darted from person to person in the room, made it obvious she was trying to figure out where all the tension radiated from. "I offered you as a bonding mate, Marika. As long as you get pregnant in a timely manner, then I figure you won't mind if they keep their little human toy.

"What!" Her shocked look couldn't be faked, and Mai suddenly felt sorry for the other woman.

Vencel moved across the room in a blur, and Timur flew back against the wall. "That's it. You will leave our presence and never come back. I will not have my mate insulted in this way."

"What the hell is going on?" The woman stomped forward placing herself between Vencel and her father. Both hands rose up. "I apologize for my father's rudeness. It is no excuse, I realize, but he has become very narrow-minded in his old age."

"He's been like that since before you were born, Marika." Gaspar tucked Mai under his arm, but she suspected he wanted to keep as much space between her and the other two werewolves as possible.

Marika came over and offered Mai a hand. Heart beating wildly, Mai stood tall and shook hers. "I do apologize for the insult my father gave to you, and I suspect by the tension in the room when I walked in, it wasn't the first one. Please accept my deepest, heartfelt congratulations on finding your mates. I wish you many peaceful years."

She shook Gaspar's and then turned and shook Vencel's hand. "Please know you are always welcome in the Bükk pack. I hope you will bring your mate to visit your homeland."

"I appreciate your offer, but I can't foresee a visit anytime soon." As he spoke, Vencel moved to stand close to Mai. He didn't stand directly in front of her but close enough to prevent anyone from having a chance of hurting her.

"We are trying hard to overcome the old and outdated traditions. But there has been some resistance from the older pack members." Marika glanced over at her unconscious father. Mai had to wonder at what kind of parent would trade away his daughter's life with such ease. The way Marika looked at her father, Mai didn't think that she carried much respect for him.

"I will collect our belongings and head back home as soon as possible. Again, I apologize for the insult to both of you and your mate.

"Thank you." Vencel reached over and clasped Mai's hand, Gaspar took the other one.

"It was nice to meet you, Mai. I hope that we get a chance to get to know each other."

"That would be nice, Marika. I would be interested in learning about your pack traditions."

"It would be in everyone's best interests if the Bükk pack stays away from our mate, Marika."

"I understand your concerns, Gaspar, and I will make certain your wishes are known."

There were no more niceties when then left. Vencel looked furious as he moved down the hall, his claws still extended from between his fingers. They were thick as a finger at the base, but then they tapered down to a lethal tip. Mai reached up a finger and stroked the length of one. Strangely, she didn't feel a single moment of fear touching such a wicked-looking weapon.

"I swear you're going to get the spanking I've been promising you." Gaspar's words shocked her out of her claw fascination

"What did I do?"

"Why would you step in front of me like that? Do you know what kind of danger you could have been in?"

"I can imagine, but I wasn't about to let her look the two of you over like that. It pissed me off." Mai tried to pull away from Gaspar, but he wouldn't allow her to. Instead, they walked more quickly down the hallway and out into the lobby. Vencel lead them, and Gaspar stayed close to her back. "Are there any more?"

She could see Vencel's head shake a negative. "I don't smell anyone. Gaspar?"

"No, we're in the clear. They have more wolves with them, but they aren't stalking us right now, and Mai's behavior will make them think twice before doing anything. I imagine they will steer clear for now. They know where we live."

"Why would you say I'll make them think twice?"

"Because you're human and nowhere near as strong as us. Since you were willing to step in front of me and glare Marika down, they will have reason to question what other talents you have."

Vencel glared over his shoulder at his brother. "Explain to me why I'm not driving my fist in your face for letting her put herself in that much danger? Why didn't you stop her Gaspar?"

"Because it's never a bad thing for someone like that to think twice before attacking."

Fear gripped Mai's heart at the possibility that they might be attacked. What if either of them got hurt trying to protect her?

"I'm going to go and have a quick talk with Albert." Vencel stopped and pulled Mai into his arms for a quick kiss. "I'll meet you at the shack.

Gaspar wrapped his arm around her shoulder and led her out into the sun. "What's the shack?"

"It's a small restaurant a few doors down. That's where the hotel gets its room service. You'll love it. It's where we go when it's Vencel's turn to cook."

Mai felt the tension disappear from her shoulders. Gaspar wouldn't make jokes if they were still in danger.

"Is it that Vencel can't cook or doesn't want to?"

"A bit of both, which works out because I hate to clean and he is almost OCD about keeping everything tidy."

Mai wasn't certain how she would fit in to their lives or if it was too soon to be even thinking that way. That Timur Denescz certainly wasn't impressed with her being with them. She glanced around her as they walked and took a good look at the town of Ecstasy Lake. It wasn't a big place by any means, but it looked pretty. They passed a candy shop and an ice cream parlor before reaching the restaurant. She could live here. It felt so peaceful, even with the groups of people milling about the small main street. Should she even be thinking this way? What if this didn't work out with Gaspar and Vencel? Maybe she should be looking more at a larger town or city?

"I can practically hear you stressing about something, Mai. Don't worry so much." Gaspar opened the door of a small building and pressed his hand to her lower back as he led her in.

The smell of fresh baked mince pies hit her senses and made her mouth water. "Oh, it smells so good in here."

"I know. Wait till Vencel catches up with us and watch his face when he walks in here."

An older woman called out to them as soon as they entered. "Welcome home, Gaspar." She looked over Mai and her smile grew. "I hope you and your brother are planning to stay around for a bit now."

Mai looked around the restaurant as they moved to a table by the window. Painted in soft colors and floral wall paper, it looked more like a quaint tea shop then a shack.

"It's a good possibility, Catherine. I'd like you to meet Mai Bennett. Vencel and I are trying to convince her to stay up here with us."

Mai felt her cheeks heat up with Gaspar's open announcement about their sharing her? She could feel her anxiety start to claw its way to the surface. What if this woman thought terrible things about her? It's a small town. She could say things that would make the entire town look at her in disgust.

"Mai, are you okay?" Gaspar's hand felt so warm when he wrapped his hand around hers.

"Sweetheart, you just lost all your color. You stay put. I know what will fix you up. Is your brother joining you two?"

"He'll be here in a second."

Mai pressed her hand against her cheek, feeling how chilled her fingers were. She could feel the wave of nausea threatening to overtake her and that last thing she wanted to do was eat.

"I don't need anything, I'm really not hungry. Thank you anyways."

But, Catherine had already moved away and if she heard Mai, she didn't give any indication. She was about to repeat herself when Gaspar scooped her up and sat down with her in his lap. He wrapped his strong arms around her, and she felt the agonizing strains of panic start to unravel.

A few people snickered and looked over at them. Mai felt their stares burning into her. "Put me down. You're making people stare."

"So let them. I don't care about them. I care about you."

"But they're going to think…"

Warm hands cupped her flushed cheeks, and she looked up into Gaspar's face. "I don't care what they think. I care what you and Vencel think. You two are important to me in my life. No one living in this town will bat an eye at your being in my lap, and the rest are simply tourists. We get a lot of them this time of year."

"I'm sorry." Mai felt terrible because she often worried about what others thought about her.

"Mai, you have nothing to apologize. What happened a moment ago? Panic attack?"

She nodded against his neck and inhaled his unique scent. Damn, the man smelled good, and the last remaining tendrils of anxiety disappeared. "It wasn't that bad and I'm feeling better now."

"I'm not. I need to hold you a bit more." She could feel him rub his cheek against the top of her head.

"Do you know why now?"

Mai shrugged her shoulders slightly.

"I'm sorry if what I said to Catherine embarrassed you."

"I don't want her to think I'm a bad person."

Gaspar leaned back a bit and encouraged her to look up at him. "*Angalom*, do you feel that way being with Vencel and me?"

"No, not at all, but other people might think…"

"Don't worry about them. You have no control over what other people think and never will. If they have issues, then it's their problem, not yours." He darted a quick kiss against her lips. "I know Vencel and I haven't shown you much of Ecstasy Lake, but it's a special place. Oh, here he is, watch him"

Mai glanced over at the door as the bell rang as it opened. Vencel strapped in and stopped dead in the doorway. She watched as he took a deep breath and then his lips curled into a goofy looking grin.

Mai covered her mouth and tried not to laugh. She didn't want to make Vencel feel bad by laughing at him.

"He does that every time we come in here. Doesn't matter if there is a lineup of people coming or going. He stops and smells for Catherine's sausage rolls."

"Because she makes the best ones I've ever tasted." Vencel reached out for Mai's hands when he reached the table. Pulling her to her feet and then into his lap after he sat down.

"Vencel. What are you doing?" Remembering what Gaspar said, Mai didn't bother to look around at any of the people in the shop. If they had an issue, then it would be their problem.

Vencel wrapped his arms around her and gave her a hug. Immediately, she felt safe and secure, as if everything in the world was right again. Gaspar stretched out his legs and relaxed in his seat. "So did you find out anything from Albert?"

"Who's Albert?" Mai tried to ignore the urge to lean against Vencel.

"He works at the hotel. Not much happens around here that he doesn't know about. The room we met them in was rented this morning. They're staying in a house a few miles outside of town. He promised to keep an eye on our guests for us. If anymore show up or they all leave at once, he will give us a call."

Catherine came over with a couple of beers and a mug of what looked like green tea. Mai loved green tea.

"Oh that's better, you're back to red and lavender." Catherine put the mug and a plate with a number of round sausage-like slices on it in front of her.

"My skin?"

"No, honey, your aura of course. Now I've made you a bit of black pudding. That will give you a bit of a boost. You eat up and let your boys take care of you. You need to put on a bit of weight. You're much too thin."

Catherine placed a plate of sausage rolls and beer in front of each of the men. "Thank you, my darling Catherine." Vencel smiled up at her, and she patted his and Gaspar's shoulders.

"You three are always welcome. Now make certain Mai eats up and I'll see you for dinner once all the excitement you have going on settles down."

For the second time in her life, Mai felt as though the world shifted on its axis. She glanced at both men who smiled down at her. "Come on, Mai. You heard what Catherine said."

"I think I want to hear more about this town."

* * * *

Marika paced back and forth along the cheap carpet that lined her hotel room floor. She glanced down at her father in disgust. *What the hell was his thinking approaching the twins like that?*

"Would someone wake him up?" She waved a hand at the six wolves that stood inside the room. They were running perimeter checks when the Solfalvi twins left. She didn't want them to know how many wolves she had with her, so she recalled them.

One of the guards walked over and lifted her father's form. The other patted his cheek much lighter than she would have. The old man jerked awake and shook his head as if it still rung. Given the size of Vencel's fist, that was a possibility. "Would you mind telling me what the fuck you were trying to prove there?"

"Don't speak to me like that, child. I'm tired of skulking the shadows like a beaten pup. I thought for certain that once the boys were shown the error of their ways, they would happily join us and come home."

"You stupid old man." She spat at his feet. "You are not here to think or offer opinions." Grabbing a white ceramic vase off a side table, Marika hurled it against the nearest wall. "They were supposed to be mine, and now you have fucked it up! You honestly think I would allow them to have a human toy?" She shuddered. "That's disgusting. If they want a mistress or two, then they can fuck some of the pack's omegas."

Another piece of cheap pottery flew across the room. "If you had done as you were told and stayed out of their way, I could have seduced them away from the weak, little human. Now they're on their guard."

Her father rose to his feet, his body more unstable than it should be. Even werewolves weren't immune to addiction, and her father's drinking long ago moved from social to a deep down need. "You're acting like a spoiled, immature bitch." He poured himself a generous serving of the cognac from the snifter on the table. "Couldn't you smell their scent all over her? If they aren't bonded by now, they will be shortly." He tilted his head back and swallowed the contents in one smooth, practiced move. Refilling his glass, he repeated the process twice more.

"Then the pathetic little human dies. What does it matter? It's not like they will be *bonded mates* with a dirty biped. With her gone, I can console the twins and bring them back to the pack. They will want to get as far away from her memory as possible, and why not run home to lick their wounds and mourn their loss?"

"I think you might be underestimating the human. She knows what we are but still didn't hesitate to step in front of the boy and challenge you."

"She is lucky I didn't tear her eyes out for that insult." Marika marched over and poured herself a liberal glass as well. As if the human could pose any shred of competition. Bad haircut, stubby, bitten nails, and pasty skin, not to forget she looked far too skinny to withstand a good fucking. Marika looked in the mirror and fluffed her perfect hair. That human didn't have a chance when compared to her. Marika clenched the crystal snifter in her hand and carried it over to her side of the room. The last thing she wanted to deal with at the moment was her father getting drunk and causing a scene. "The only thing that stopped me is I promised myself I'll tear her throat out and watch her drown in her own blood."

She could feel a smile curve her lips when she visualized the blood spurting from the human's neck in time to her heartbeats.

"It will have to look like as accident."

"We'll make it a good accident." She held up her hand and allowed her manicured claws to break out from the ends of her fingers. "I want to play with her a bit before I kill her."

Chapter Twelve

Mai lay in bed and listened to the soft morning of the forest around them. One of the guys must have left the windows open last night. A soft breeze floated over them, and the rising sun shone warm on their legs. She didn't remember coming to bed last night. Neither Vencel nor Gaspar were in very good moods, and she wasn't entirely certain her presence helped matters.

They both brooded and gave short answers to any questions. But when she tried to excuse herself to her room, Gaspar scooped her up and carried her to the couch. She spent the next few hours watching TV curled up next to Vencel, with Gaspar's head in her lap. Neither of them talked much and didn't joke around at all, but then she got the impression they didn't want to let her go anywhere alone. Last thing she remembered was asking Vencel to put her cup of tea on the side table before laying her head against his chest.

Lying partially on her side, she leaned back against Vencel's large body. His left arm stretched out over the pillows, and her head rested in the crook. Gaspar's head rested on her chest below her collarbone. She could feel his warm breath against her breast. She didn't have any covers, but being sandwiched between two large male bodies kept her warm enough. Both men gave off enough body heat that she suspected that she might never need to use a blanket to sleep again.

Her brain froze when she realized she thought in forever terms with them. As far as she knew, this might be a fling for them. Given Gaspar's former career, she didn't think it could last. She could never share her men with anyone else and didn't see herself able to keep them both interested in the long run. Maybe she was overthinking this entire situation? She should go with the flow and enjoy it as it came. At least she would have good memories after they left.

Men like them didn't stay with weak women. They were too strong, and she might never be confident enough to handle that. Oh hell, when they walked down the street and some woman made a pass at them. Just the thought of it made her angry. She should find herself someone more like her, safe and, well, boring.

"We don't like what you are thinking, *Nyuszikam*." Vencel stirred behind her. She felt him run his hand over her hair and tuck some behind her ear. She tried to look at his face without disturbing Gaspar too much. *How could he know my thoughts?* Gaspar still looked like he was sleeping.

"Your scent changes when you start to worry and get upset." Gaspar's words vibrated against her skin. He snuggled against her body and wrapped his arm over her hip. "Whatever it is that's bothering you, Vencel and I will fix it for you. Don't worry."

Mai smiled. They were so arrogant. The only way to fix it would be for her to leave them, and she wanted to cry at the idea. A sharp pain in her chest followed that thought, and both the men growled deep in their chests.

Gaspar lifted his head and met her gaze. "What's wrong?"

"What makes you think something is wrong?" Mai tried to keep her voice steady, but right now she felt so uncertain of everything.

"Because whatever you're thinking of made you sad." Vencel ran his fingers through her hair again. "Tell us and we'll fix it for you."

"You make it sound so easy."

"Because it is easy. There isn't anything we can't fix for you."

"But I'm the one broken. You can't fix me."

Gaspar pushed himself up on one elbow. "You realize that you are ours right. We lo…adore you just as you are. There isn't a thing wrong with you and the sooner you realize that…"

Vencel cupped her cheek and turned her face toward him. "The sooner we can bond with you and make you ours forever."

"Bond? What the hell is that?" She struggled to wiggle out from between the two of them, but they wouldn't let her move. She felt Vencel's cock hardening against her bum. He jerked his hips slightly increasing the pressure. It brought back so many feelings from the night before. She could feel her body responding, flooding with moisture again.

Gaspar growled above her and splayed his hand over her lower stomach. "No, stay here and talk." The only thoughts in Mai's head were in regard to how close his fingers were to her clit. A few inches more and she could rub herself against him.

"I can't talk to you both like this. I get distracted."

"I can tell." Vencel nuzzled her temple with his lips. "You smell so good." He shifted his hips behind her again, sliding his hardening cock against space between the globes of her ass.

Above her, Gaspar's lips curled into a wicked grin. "I know firsthand how delicious you taste as well." He traced a finger around one of her nipples watching it as it tightened up into a bud.

A remembered image of Gaspar between her legs the other day flooded her memories. "Stop trying to distract me." She smacked at Gaspar's hand but missed and smacked herself on the tit. A shock ran though her body at the sensation, and she couldn't help the gasp that escaped her lips.

Vencel grabbed her hand and anchored it above her head. "Oh no you don't, naughty girl. We are going to have to explore that side of you later."

Gaspar grabbed her other hand and pinned it to the bed as he went back to teasing her nipples. "I bet she would love to have the extra sensation of a spanking."

"I would not." Mai was both intrigued by the idea and equally determined not to let it happen. They had too much control over her body, and she didn't want to give them any more ammunition.

Vencel pushed a knee between her legs and then raised it and hooked her leg on the other side of his. Lifting his knee bared her pussy for Gaspar's easy viewing. Gaspar reached down and smacked her lightly right on her clit. Mai jerked at the sharp sensation as need flooded her body along with a creamy moisture between her legs.

"Oh yeah, *Angyalom*. Look at you reacting to a little smack." He swirled a finger around her folds and then brought the wet digit to his lips. "I'm going to give you a proper spanking while Vencel holds on to you. I bet you come so hard, we'll have to change the sheets." He slipped his finger into his mouth and sucked it clean. "You taste so good. I don't think I will ever get enough."

Gaspar leaned down and kissed her. Slipping his tongue between her lips to play with hers, allowing her to taste herself on him. She tugged at her trapped hands, but neither man would allow her to go. Something about being helpless to do anything but what they wanted created a feeling of peace inside her. No matter what they did, she knew she could trust them. Gaspar rubbed her clit with the pad of his fingers, grazing the sensitive skin so softly she could hardly feel it. Vencel angled his hips, and she could feel the broad tip of him press against her opening.

"Are you too sore?" She could feel herself stretching to accommodate his girth, a slight ache, but the sensation of him moving in short little slides overpowered any pain. "I'm fine." She felt a tremor run along her limbs.

Vencel must have felt it to because he nipped her on the shoulder. "You're squeezing me like a vice *Nyuszikam.*"

"You should see her from this angle, brother. Next time we switch places. Her skin is flushed, and her pretty pussy is swollen and so wet. Her nipples are like pencil erasers." He bent down and flicked his tongue over her nipples. Mai jerked in Vencel's arms. Gaspar's tongue felt rough against her sensitive skin.

"Mai, we want you to stay here." Vencel splayed his hand across her lower stomach, a hot brand against her skin. She felt him roll his hips before plunging deeper within her. "Stay here with us."

Gaspar kissed a path between her breasts while he spoke. "We want to take care of you and have you in our lives." The idea sounded like heaven to her. *Maybe too good?*

"For a while?" Concentrating on what they were saying seemed almost impossible. The way they made her feel stole all her concentration. She pushed at Gaspar's waist until he got the hint and moved up higher until his cock was in line with her lips.

Gaspar shuddered when she brushed a finger over the tip of his cock. Vencel slipped in and out her in a steady rhythm. She licked the plum head and caught a few drops that gathered in the small slit. "Oh yeah, slip my cock between your lips."

She smiled up at him and sucked the head of his cock past her lips. She shuttled up and down the length of him, playing with the heavy sac hanging between his legs.

"You are doing incredible, Mai." Vencel's deep voice encouraged her on. Taking him deeper into her throat, Vencel adjusted his strokes to match the rhythm she moved. She started to feel the tightening of Gaspar's balls under her fingers when he suddenly pulled away from her lips with an audible pop.

The men rolled with her until Vencel lay on his back, and she straddled his hips. His hands gripped her waist, and he pulled her down against him, grinding up against her. Gaspar cupped her face in his hands and kissed her soundly, pressing his thick cock against her lower belly.

Vencel slipped from her body, and she felt a cooling sensation on the rosette of her bottom. "A little lube…" Feeling him circle the sensitive area lit every one of Mai's nerves on fire. He played with her back hole, pressing the lube inside her, the sensations driving her insane. The tight ring of muscles protested, but she concentrated on relaxing.

"That's perfect, *Nyuszikam*, let me into that tight ass of yours." He gripped her tightly around the waist, slowing her descent on his length. Mai gripped Vencel's forearms to steady herself. She felt too stretched but at the same time wanted more.

"You'll get more, *Angyalom*, we promise." Gaspar kissed her until she sat completely on Vencel's cock. "Now it's my turn." Vencel sat up and encouraged Mai to lean slightly back against him. Gaspar moved between her legs and pierced her core with his length. With her legs trapped on either side of Vencel's, she had no choice but to take them.

It frightened her and aroused her at the same time. They controlled her movements, allowing her bursts of heat and then held onto her hips and made her remain still.

"I can't..." Mai panted, lost in a sea of sensations. "Please, move"

It almost felt as if she could feel each of them deep inside her soul. She mentally reached for something she didn't understand.

"Forever, *Angyalom*, we want forever. Never leave us."

"*Nyuszikam*, be our mate. Stay with us."

They bit her on either side of her neck sending a white-hot wave of heat blasting through her. No pain but exquisite acceptance, her body felt as if a swath of fur rushed over it. Each layer from the firm bristles to the soft undercoat caressed her skin. Her body strained for more but couldn't quite reach...

"Yes, forever." With those words, her body flood with heat bursting through her nerves and pores, vibrating her body with its intensity. Vencel and Gaspar rocked in and out of her body in perfect tandem. Their movements as wild as the creatures hidden inside them. Mai felt her soul tear in three and then come back together. Cracks filled in where she didn't realize any existed.

The music of howling surrounded her, and she screamed out in harmony.

Chapter Thirteen

Mai stood under a generous spray of hot water. Her body felt sore and achy, but she couldn't deny the incredible feeling of peace that filled her. As if she didn't have a worry in the world. That alone should concern her, but the unexplainable sense of being exactly where she should be overrode her normal tendency to overthink her worries. Accompanying this feeling of "rightness" was the urge to press the twins for information. Exactly what did this bonding thing Vencel spoke about mean to her? *Or was it nothing more than words to make me feel special?*

She hurried through the rest of her shower and then quickly donned a tank top and cut off shorts. A moment of wickedness came over her, and she deliberately left her bra in the suitcase. Glancing at herself, she almost changed her mind. Her nipples pushed in sharp relief against the fabric. The bite marks they gave her earlier stood out like a beacon on her pale skin. A small, negative voice in the back of her head reminded her that they remained out her league. Why even dream of a future with them? Now that they both got what they wanted, would she find herself pointed back to the city and her lonely life in front of a computer?

"Fuck that," she said to her reflection in the mirror. Last night was more than incredible sex. She didn't have words for what happened, but she'd bet the twins knew. Feeling more than a little determined, she marched downstairs in search of them. She was going to get a solid answer from them because the idea that this might be nothing but a fling made her feel like her heart was about to break.

* * * *

"You pushed the issue, *Angyalom*."

"You wanted to know what we wanted." Vencel didn't sound like himself. Hell, he didn't even sound human. Mai backed up, her hand on the deck railing to guide her. The conversation didn't go anything like she mentally planned. In fact, they both seemed to get angrier every time she mentioned going back to her apartment.

Gaspar stepped to the right as if he planned to cut off her escape. Her heart beat a rapid pulse in her chest, and she could almost feel the adrenaline begin to pump though her.

"All I want is for you to tell me the truth. I know I'm not strong enough for you. All I want is for you to admit it."

A low warning snarl vibrated from Gaspar, he bared his teeth at her. Teeth which looked much sharper than they did moments ago.

"Do you really think any of us have a choice in this?"

"But Marika said..." Vencel smacked the wood railing, the sudden sound made Mai jump.

"I don't care about anything that bitch has to say. She has no part of this conversation. You, on the other hand, are very much part of it."

"What do you mean we don't have a choice?"

"Do you want to leave us, Mai?

NO! Every cell in her body revolted at that possibility, but her conscious mind realized that sometimes life didn't have happy endings.

This is your chance, *Nyuszikam*." Both he and Gaspar stepped closer, blocking off her escape route. "Run."

The dark, sexual tone to Vencel's voice made Mai's body want to drop to her knees and nuzzle her cheek against his hardening cock. *What the hell was going on here?*

"I don't understand. You want me to leave?"

"We want you to run, Mai." Vencel placed his face in front of hers, his nose inches away. "Try to get away from us. If you can, we'll let you go."

Gaspar stepped in and licked a path along her neck to her ear. He nipped sharply at her earlobe. "But if we catch you, you are ours to do what we want to. There will be no escaping us, ever."

A dark downy fur broke out over Vencel's skin. And fear rushed through Mai like a tidal wave. If he was this close to losing it, he could kill her, even accidentally.

"Run, little rabbit."

Mai's body flooded with adrenaline as she slipped past Gaspar and started running across their expansive backyard. She darted a look over her shoulder and nearly tripped. Each man stared at her with an intensity that terrified her. She was the sole focus of their attention. Her body responded with a rush of heat between her legs. She knew they would catch her, and she wanted them to, but she didn't want to make it easy for them. Turning her attention to the trees ahead of her, she planned her route. With their sense of smell, hiding would be an impossibility. She had to outsmart them. She remembered the river that wasn't too far away. If she could get there, she could duck under the water and swim in any direction. They wouldn't be able to find her right away. She wanted to prove to them that she had the strength to be with them. That despite the fact the she was human, she did have her talents. Marika might be a better match for them, but Mai was the one who loved them. She had to prove it first.

A small, dark voice in the back of her thoughts asked why she wanted to hide when getting caught would be so much better. Mai paused as she reached the tree line, darting a quick look over her shoulder in time to see Vencel leap over the porch railing and land solid on his feet. It wasn't that fact that he jumped but the speed and grace he exhibited in the move. Gaspar tilted back his head and howled long into the sky. Mai pushed past the tree line and hoped that they didn't decide to cheat. She glanced back a few times and could just make out the two of them still standing by the house. Vencel paced back and forth, while Gaspar looked to have hopped onto the railing and crouched there. She knew she couldn't be easily seen, but it felt like Gaspar's gaze burned a hole between her shoulder blades. Once she ran down a small incline and out of their view, she changed her direction and ran toward the river.

She stumbled once when the sound of a wolf's howl echoed through the trees, matched by a second voice. Heart pounding, the sound vibrated through her chest, bringing a wave of moisture between her legs. That must be her warning. They were coming. Not used to running like this, Mai's legs were already starting to burn. A twig snapped to her left so she darted to the right, continuing on. They couldn't run super fast through the forest and not make a sound. That was impossible. *Right?* She could hear the water a few feet away. A large tree had fallen over its bank, so Mai hopped up on it and ran its length. A quick look over her shoulder revealed that they hadn't caught up with her yet. Knowing she only had a few moments to spare, she crawled to the end of the tree. Holding onto the branches, she allowed herself to slip into the water with the least amount of noise possible.

* * * *

Gaspar ran through the underbrush with his brother only a few feet away. Mai's scent glittered like a shining beacon to him. Vencel barked and raced forward. Apparently Mai enjoyed this little game as well. He could smell the changes to her scent in the air. Her arousal grew with every yard she ran. By the time they caught up with her, she would be soaked. His body felt primed, and when he caught her he would shift back into his human form and fuck her senseless. The aroma of her sweet pussy coated his tongue. Change of plan, he was going to bury his face between her legs before fucking her senseless. They both burst out of the trees onto the river's bank. *Clever girl.* He followed her scent along a fallen tree, where it vanished. This might buy her a few more minutes, but it wouldn't be hard to find where she broke the surface. With a quick nod to his brother, the men split up and headed in opposite directions along the bank. She couldn't have gotten too far ahead of them. Gaspar's sure footing lent him a burst of speed, but he couldn't see her or hear her breathing. Neither could he sense Vencel's burst of joy when finding her. Vencel felt the same as him, frustrated with a tough of fear clouding the edges. *Where did she go?*

The beginning of fear tainted the edge of his arousal at the possibility of her being hurt. Vencel already plunged into the calm river, swimming to the other side. Gaspar followed him, and they both ran opposite directions along the banks on that side. He ran up river, scenting the ground along the river's edge searching for anything that might point him in a direction. There were lots of animal scents but nothing human.

Human thoughts crowded out the animal within, and he shifted back into human form. "Mai!" His voice rang out along the river and echoed in the trees. With his heart pounding, he spun around. If she suddenly appeared laughing because she tricked him, he was going to spank her ass until she screamed. Right after kissing her in relief. A burst of fear from his brother almost drove him to his knees, and he shifted back into his wolf form and sped back.

He found Vencel running in circles around an area down river and just around the bend. The scent of several wolves and Mai mixed together. There was also the tang of blood in the air. Both of them growled as they sped in the direction the scents traveled. Cresting a small incline the scents grew stronger, but so did that of automobile exhaust. A slight squawk of tires drew them both out of the cover of the trees. A large SUV sped down the country road away from them. They both bolted off after the truck, but it quickly out sped them and turned onto a main road where both men lost track of the scent with all the other cars.

Vencel howled a sound of desperation and pain. Gaspar joined his voice to his brother's before they both turned back to the shelter of the trees, running off to the house. The forest around their home fell silent in reaction to the agitation of two predators. They both felt the same thing at this moment, aside from the deep-rooted need to get their mate back. They wanted retribution against those that had come after them.

The air shimmered around each of them as they reached the porch, shifting to human form they ran up the stairs on human feet. Quickly pulling on the clothes they pulled off a short time ago, they tore off the porch and to the truck. Vencel drove like a man possessed, kicking up a cloud of dust and stone as he bounced down the small dirt road. Gaspar gripped the handle above his door with one hand, the other braced the dash. His breakneck speed caused more than one horn to honk in his directions when he screeched on to the main road. Gaspar sat in the passenger seat, one leg bouncing with restless energy. He cracked his knuckles and occasionally smacked the dashboard.

"We need a plan."

"Really, like what?" Vencel swerved onto the shoulder and gunned past a slow-moving Charger. Whipping back onto the road in front of him. Gaspar reached over and hit the emergency flashers. At least that would warn the other drives slightly before his brother drove up their ass. "What if they took her somewhere else?"

"Then we kill whoever is there right after we make the last one talk."

Gaspar hadn't seen his brother this focused since the war. They tried not to get involved with the human's struggle for power but neither would they allow them to be slaughtered needlessly. They helped who they could cross the border, slaughtering the enemy patrols that had a penchant to shoot first and fuck the rest.

He continued to phone their rooms every minute, but no one answered. He demanded answers from the front desk, but all they would say is that the rooms had not been checked out of. The twenty-minute drive to the hotel felt like forever. Best-case scenario, Timur's men only had a ten-minute lead on them. Ten minutes in which the worst things could happen to their mate. "They will kill her if they realize we have bonded with her. We should have waited until they left the country."

Vencel darted a sharp look over at him. Okay, little too late for this realization, but he didn't care. Mai didn't feel like she'd been forced into anything, and now they had their True Mate.

"It wouldn't have changed anything. The caught us with our pants down. I didn't even scent the air before we let her hit the trees."

"They aren't that stupid, Vencel. Neither of us noticed in wolf form either. They must have had surveillance up wind."

"We should have taken better care of her."

"We will. They won't kill her, not right away."

"What makes you so certain?"

"Because if I don't believe that, I will lose my mind." He took a deep breath and tried to push the animal instincts to shift and start spilling blood. "Okay, they want us. She will be used as a hostage."

Vencel took a deep breath and tried to calm himself. Gaspar reached over and placed his hand on his brother's shoulder, aiding him in his attempt to calm himself. The one advantage they had could easily be a disadvantage. Their closeness could escalate their panic, each feeding off the other. A flicker of warmth tickled his senses.

"What the fuck was that?" Vencel jerked the wheel to keep them on the road.

"Fuck, Ven. Watch the road already. If you kill us both, we won't be any good to her." He closed his eyes and tried to understand what brushed against their senses. The faint flicker concentrated on the bright spot inside him. A small light gently protected within his chest, the beginnings of their bond.

"Vencel." Gaspar couldn't believe it. "It's Mai. There are already the beginnings of a bond with her. It's slight, but it's there." He poured as much love as he could into that light. It felt cold and confused, but he could fee her grabbling for any sense of him. "Vencel?"

"I know I can feel her. I'm trying not to get us killed here. Keep ahold of her spirit, keep contact with her, and let her know we are coming."

Angyalom, we're coming. Hold on little rabbit. We're coming.

It would take much longer than a day for their bond to be strong enough for her to hear them, but for now this would have to do. He couldn't hear her, but he knew she felt him. The panicked flickering eased slightly. He could taste her fear in the back of his throat, but then it could easily be his own fear trying to choke him. He felt Vencel's love for her pulse with his against the faint strain.

"Do you think she knows it's us?"

"Yes, somehow, I don't know how, but I think she knows. I wish the bond was strong enough so she could tell us where she is."

"At this point I'm happy to know that she is alive. She feels scared and confused, but I don't think she is in any pain."

Chapter Fourteen

Mai lay inside the trunk of a car. She never felt so terrified in her entire life. Hot tears coursed down her cheeks as she tried to wriggle out of her bonds. Everything happened so fast. She felt so brave slipping into the water and swimming downstream. She wanted to get a bit of a head start on the twins, but to be honest she didn't really want to get too far ahead. So she swam around the bend, just out of sight and then crawled out of the river. Soaking wet would slow her down some, but perhaps she wouldn't be wearing these clothes too long. She managed to crawl over the rock and looked over her shoulder expecting to see one of them on the other side of the river. Turning back, she came face-to-face with a large man she wished she didn't recognize.

"Well, this is convenient."

She never had time to scream before the world turned black.

When she came to, Mai thought she might be dead. She couldn't see anything, but slowly her senses came back to her. She could smell exhaust and something rattled around behind her. *Oh please, don't let it be a body.* Raising her wrists to her mouth she tried to bite at her restraints. It felt like a plastic tie held her hands together, and her ankles must be bound the same way. So much for Gaspar's idea. Perhaps if they didn't see her as such a threat, they wouldn't have secured her to well.

Voices argued inside the car, but she couldn't make out what they were saying. *Okay, be quiet, but don't just lay here.* Mai remember reading once about a woman who was trapped in a trunk. She broke the back light out and waved down help. Anything would be better than lying here waiting to find out her fate. If she lay there any longer, she would end up lost in a panic attack of grand mal proportions.

Mai carefully slid herself to the trunk and felt around with her hands, only feeling carpeting beneath her fingers. Following the edge she tried to pick at the material and pull it off the frame. Her fingers ached, and she bent back almost every nail before she gave up. Closing her eyes, she tried to envision her men and wished she could see them. She had to believe they would come for her, but how would they find her?

Fear and panic pushed at her thoughts. *Gaspar, Vencel, where are you?* She curled up and tried to think of them and not panic. The harder she thought about them, the more she could feel them with her. *Please help.* A warmth lay over her troubled thoughts like a blanket. She could almost feel them stroking her hair and her back, reassuring her that they were coming. She lay still and didn't move for fear of losing the sensation. Even if this was all in her imagination, she didn't want to lose it.

The car turned and bounced down a side road that felt worse than the one leading to their home. It jarred her, and she lost the connection to them. At least now she felt a bit better and not as panicked. The car stopped, and she heard car doors opening. Two slams shuddered through the vehicle. So she was about to face at least two people, one of them the jerk who took her. Despite her attempts to look strong, hot tears escaped and trailed into her ear. Footsteps walked along the edge of the car, while the other sounded like it moved away. A key in the lock and then the truck lid lifted. Sunlight streamed in as did the fresh air. Mai breathed deep before looking up into the face of her kidnapper. It was the same man who grabbed her on the river's edge.

"Please let me go." A shiver racked her body. The cool breeze over her wet clothes didn't help.

"I'm sorry. I can't." He gripped Mai by the shoulders and flipped her over his shoulder and then headed into the house.

"All secure." Another male voice had Mai lifting her head, but she didn't recognize this man. He looked at her with a curiosity that made Mai nervous. As long as they thought of her as a dirty human, she didn't have to worry about them touching her. She glared at him and gave him her filthiest look. "They will kill you both for what you are doing."

All emotion drained from his gaze. "They will try."

He carried her into a small cottage and dropped onto a soft bed. The man flicked open a large knife, and Mai scrambled back away from him. "I'm not going to cut you. You won't need these anymore." He pinned her arms down and ran the knife's edge along the plastic tie, repeating he process with her ankles. Mai immediately started to rub the abrasions on her skin. They stung, but not as bad as she expected.

"Bathroom is there." He pointed to a small door to the left. "Stay here, and please don't do anything that will make me hurt you." He got up and stalked out of the room. Mai slipped from the bed and immediately moved over to the door and tried the handle. It turned, but the door wouldn't open. They must have locked it from the other side. Next she tried the only window, but it looked to be painted shut. Fear hammered at her again as she moved over to sit on the bed. For a moment she thought about getting out of her wet clothes, but what good would that do her? The last thing she wanted was for one of them to come in while she stood there in nothing but a sheet.

She checked out the bathroom. It was clean and had a supply of fresh towels. She thought that perhaps she could lock herself in there, but the door didn't have a lock, and there was nothing in the medicine cabinet either. No mirror to smash and only a small vent in the ceiling. If she stepped on the sink, she might be able to reach it, but she would never be able to squeeze out.

One thing was for certain—she wasn't going to sit here and wait to be killed.

* * * *

Vencel shot up the drive to the large A-frame house that the Hungarian wolves had rented. A Mercedes sat outside the building, but there weren't any other vehicles. Gaspar has the door open and already jumped out before Vencel completely stopped.

"Don't kill anyone without me!" He threw the truck in park and followed a moment behind his brother. Unlike the other day, there wasn't anyone waiting at the door, unfortunately. His wolf rode him hard, and he wanted to tear out someone's throat. Following the only scents available, they headed into the main room. As soon as they cleared the doorway, a symphony of clicks warned them that several guns were pointed in their direction. Stupid, Vencel could smell the gun oil the moment they cleared the door. Timur Denescz sat in a large chair facing them with his bodyguards flanking him on either side. "Gentlemen. Don't do anything stupid."

"Oh, what you did is stupid." Gaspar snarled

"What we're going to do to you isn't," Vencel finished. He knew he could take a few shots before they dropped him, and he would take out as many of them as possible in the process.

"I know we have a difference in opinion. If you want your human, then stay out of our way. You come on our soil, and she will be hunted as will you both."

Vencel's confusion echoed the same feeling from Gaspar. "We had no intentions of coming back. You made the first move in our territory."

They both stepped forward, and the bodyguards pulled weapons. "You tell us where you put our mate, and we will let you go."

"You don't tell us, and we will start tearing into you." Gaspar's clawed fingers curled shut in the air.

"You think I have your dirty biped."

Vencel couldn't stop the snarl that rose up in his throat. One more insult and to hell with them all, he was going to start killing them.

Starting with the old man. Timur must have seen his death in Vencel's eyes because his scent of arrogance diminished under a rising fear.

"Where is your daughter, old man? Where did Marika go?"

The man's eyes grew wide when the situation sank in. He grabbed for his phone in his pocket and dialed a number.

"Don't tell her we are here." Gaspar snarled.

"What the fuck do you want?" Marika obviously didn't have the respect of her father that she led them to believe.

"The Solfalvi twins were here, and they have lost their toy. I want the human, Marika."

"No. I've got the pathetic female, and I am going to use her as I see fit."

"You are not the leader of this pack, child."

Marika's nasty laugh could be heard through the phone. Someone wasn't hanging onto their sanity well. "When they can't find her, they will be back. Once they are done with you, I'll be the leader by the time I touch down on our soil."

"You do not get to rule like this. You will destroy everything we have worked for."

"You don't have a clue what you are talking about. I've worked for years toward this. Of course I expected the Nazi soldiers to cut down the twins before they ever got out of the country. It's a shame really, and now we need them."

"They aren't going to do what you want."

"Yes, they will. Once they find her body and are completely destroyed with grief, I will invite them to come home. There won't be anything here for them."

It took every shred of Vencel's control not to start screaming his denial at her words. He could feel Gaspar feeding him energy to calm down. Regardless of what happened, he would rip the woman's heart out with his own claws.

"I don't plan on being here when they return. I'm not going to be your scapegoat. Whatever you do, you bring the consequences on your own head."

"Whatever. What's wrong, Daddy, sad you didn't get to kill the dirty Homo sapien yourself? Don't worry, I plan to film myself tearing her to pieces. Something to keep me warm when the nights get cold at home. That is, when I don't have one of the twins in my bed." The line went dead at that point. Timur sat there, slumped in defeat. His face looked an ashen gray, and he looked to the twins. Nodding at one of his bodyguards, the large man tossed a GPS at Gaspar.

"What is that?"

"My daughter's vehicles are lo-jacked. You can find her with this."

Gaspar quickly estimated exactly where she parked her vehicle. They had a home up here long before most of these building were built. There wasn't any building up in this part of the country they didn't know of.

"I will take my men and go home. I will stay away from here as long as you stay away from Europe."

"You aren't going anywhere." A large man sauntered into the house, wearing nothing but a pair of army shorts and a drab olive tank top. His scent flooded the room as did his status.

"See now, you are in my territory without asking permission. You have kidnapped a human in my territory and not just any human, but my friends' mate."

Vencel turned toward Gordon. "You took your time."

The Alpha shrugged one shoulder. "It's a big territory. Would you like to stay?"

Gaspar shook his head answering for both of them. "We need to find Mai."

Timur stood and look down his nose at all of them. Apparently he was finished being helpful. His guards stepped up on either side of him. "The Canadas have not formally joined the European council.

You are not organized enough to enforce anything. I do not have to follow any of your decrees."

A small corner of Gordon's mouth turned up. "I love arrogant assholes who underestimate us." A scrabble of claws alerted them to a number of animals entering the house. The soldiers that held guns on the twins quickly lowered them.

"What are you doing?" Timur growled at his wolves. "Shoot them all."

Twenty large creatures of various breeds poured into the room, teeth bared, ears pinned back. It was going to be a bloodbath.

The Hungarian wolves looked to each other and the sound of multiple weapons thudded on the floor. They recognized a no-win scenario when they saw it.

Timur growled and his hands stretched into lethal claws. "Fucking puppies, you're nothing but a bunch of worthless dogs!"

Gordon's hands morphed into deadly claws as he looked at the Hungarian leader, disgust coloring his expression. "You two find your mate. We'll take care of this."

Vencel and Gaspar didn't hesitate, and a minute later they raced down the highway. "I'll pull over by the old bridge, and then we can get out and shift from there. We can make it faster on foot than in the truck."

"I'm going to tear that bitch's face off when we catch up to her."

Gaspar hesitated for a split-second and then nodded in agreement. Marika had taken their mate from them, and for that she would face a shifter's punishment. Mates, especially True Mates, were to be cherished and protected at all costs.

* * * *

Mai perched on the top of the dresser. In her hands she held a large, heavy piece of wood post she unscrewed from the bed frame. Adrenaline pumped through her system. Her only chance to escape would be a sneak attack. Vencel's comment about sensitive muzzles gave her the idea. Who ever came through this door was going to get a surprise of their life.

Her muscles quivered when she heard the scratch of nails against the floor. Listening carefully, she determined that only one wolf paced in the other room. It stopped, and Mai strained to hear something else. The men who brought her here left shortly after locking her in. She watched two wolves run into the forest moments later. Considering she didn't have a clue when they would be back or how long they would be gone, she didn't bother to break the window and escape that way. Her only option was to try to get to the car and pray he left the keys in it.

"Little pig, little pig, let me iiiinnnnnn." Mai jerked at the first word and almost gave away her hiding place. The last word was drawn out in an off-key singsong. Anger flooded her system, driving away the fear and sharpening her senses. She reached for the string that she attached to the bathroom door and gave it a yank. The bathroom door slammed shut with an audible bang. Let the blonde bitch think Mai wanted to hide.

"I'm gonna huff and puff and..." As the door opened Mai swung the post in a hard arc aiming for the blond bitch's face. She connected with a grisly crunch and blood sprayed as Marika screamed in terror, holding her face she dropped to the floor.

Mai didn't waste any time. Leaping off the dresser she landed outside the doorway. Keeping the post gripped in her hand, she ran for the open door. *Don't look back, get to the car, don't look back...*

Knowing that her life depended on it, Mai ran as fast as her legs could handle. A low growl followed her, and she knew that Marika must be right on her heels. The car sat on the drive, but there was no chance she would make it. She ran out into the sunshine and onto the grass. Two wolves stood in front of her, blood coating their muzzles and staining their coats.

Their ears pinned back against their heads, tails stood straight up and in a moment of slow motion they leapt for her.

"Get down!" Vencel and Gaspar's combined voices echoed in her head, and Mai immediately threw herself on to the ground. There wasn't anything graceful about the move, but the thick grass eased the impact. Both wolves sailed over her, and a blood-curdling shriek filled the air. Mai didn't stop moving. Gaining her feet, she continued her race to the car that brought her here.

Her heart pounded in her throat. *Any moment I'm going to feel claws on my back.* But the attack never came. She ripped open the passenger side door and threw herself inside, slamming the door and engaging the locks. Scrambling into the driver's side, she grabbed for the keys, but nothing hung from the ignition. *NO!*

Panicked she looked through the windshield and saw two wolves fighting a naked Marika. Her face was a gory mess. She stilled clawed at the wolves, but they nimbly leapt out of the way. Mai took in a deep breath and realized that her hands weren't shaking as bad as she would have expected right now. In fact, she felt much calmer. It must be the twins' presence. Glancing out the window, she watched as the wolves appeared to be strategizing their next move as they circled. For a moment, Mai felt a moment of compassion for the other woman, until a vicious swipe of her claws almost caught Gaspar across the face. Those lethal claws that Marika wouldn't have hesitated to use on her. When Vencel leapt back to avoid a similar swipe, Marika seized the opportunity and fled in to the woods.

Mai lay down along the seat and waited for them to finish. She didn't doubt Vencel and Gaspar would win, but she didn't want to watch either. Neither did she want to be sitting in plain view if the other two wolves came back. She lay there listening waiting to hear something.

"Angyalom?"

Mai popped up and looked out, watching as both men ran across the grass, naked and soaking wet. She unlocked the car and barely had the door open before Gaspar pulled her into his embrace. His mouth, hot and demanding, burned through the last remaining webs of fear that clung to her. She wrapped her legs around Gaspar's waist and Vencel pressed his chest against her back. Trapping her between them, one of them cupped her bottom supporting her completely.

When Gaspar released her lips, she turned in his arms and Vencel immediately claimed her lips. His kiss was no less intense as his brothers, and she felt her body responding to them both. The depth of their feelings for her vibrated against her soul. She didn't understand how she felt it, but she hoped they could feel her as well.

"You were so strong, *Nyuszikam*. I'm so proud of you." Vencel pressed an urgent kiss against her temple. Both men stroked her and petted her as if they needed to make certain that she wasn't hurt.

"I'm okay." She placed one hand on each of their cheeks. "I heard you tell me to get down. Is that normal?"

"To hear us this soon, no, *Angyalom*. But, given the extreme circumstances of the day I'm not surprised." Gaspar tightened his grip around her lifting her off her feet. "Vencel, let's take our mate home."

"Wait, there are a couple more wolves in the forest that work for her."

"No, there aren't, and taking care of them is what almost prevented us from getting to you on time."

"When I think about how close you were." Gaspar buried his face in her neck and took a deep breath. Mai could feel his entire body vibrate under her hands. Vencel growled low in his throat and nuzzled the other side of her neck. She stroked and petted her men knowing that they needed reassurance. "I shouldn't ask how close she was behind me, should I?"

Neither of her men said anything, which told her more than she needed to know. She wouldn't dwell on it or even think about it because everything turned out all right in the end.

Chapter Fifteen

A low pounding disturbed Mai as she slept, pissing her off. After everything that happened, she finally got to go to sleep, and now someone had woken her up? She rubbed her eyes with the heel of her hand and looked around. Heavy blinds covered the window, and she lay in the middle of their large bed, but her men were nowhere to be seen. She frowned at the clock on the side table. It was morning already? Damn, she felt like she hadn't slept a wink. The pounding noise stopped, but she could hear low voices coming from downstairs. She pulled on Vencel's T-shirt and padded over to the door.

"Where the fuck is my sister asshole!"

Oh shit, that sounded like Marcario. What the hell was her brother doing here? Mai started down the hall but paused when she heard some shoving and grunts. Holy crap, were they fighting?

"Dude, if either of you have touched my little sister, I will have you killed and make it look like a heart attack." *That's Jelani.* Her brother worked as a nurse, so his threat wasn't completely fabricated.

She rushed down the stairs and looked over the lower half of the banister. As she suspected, both her brothers were trying to force their way in. Vencel held Jelani by his shirt, and Gaspar struggled in a grapple hold on the floor with Marcario. "What the fuck is going on here?"

"Mai, where did you learn such language?"

"Mom?" At that moment Mai wanted to drop into a large hole and hide forever. Facing her brothers while hiding behind her lovers was one thing, but to have her mother there as well? Might as well divert what trouble she could. "Marcario taught me."

"These men didn't believe that we are your brothers and didn't want to let us in." Marcario struggled against Gaspar who obviously was trying not to hurt her moronic brother.

"And the wisest solution you came up with was to force your way in?"

"Why did you let them get away with this?" She looked over the wrestling men in the doorway at her mother.

"Well, sweetheart, the boys thought you were being held against your will."

"And where the hell did you get an idea like that?"

"I talked to Stephanie." Jelani shoved at Vencel again in an attempt to get him to move.

"What! Why would she say that?"

"She didn't really. She said you went away with a couple brothers and we should leave you alone and you would call us when you got home. I knew you wouldn't do such a thing, so you must have been forced."

Mai's mother stepped up and pinched Jelani, right on the fleshy part of the back his arm.

"Ow!" He jumped and let go of Vencel to rub the spot on his arm. Mai's mother shoved her son in the ribs forcing him to move.

"You." She pointed at Marcario. "Get off that floor and stop this ridiculous outburst." Her brother immediately let go of Gaspar and got to his feet. He held out a hand, and Gaspar grabbed it helping him to his feet. "And, that's enough swearing out of you."

Vencel and Gaspar moved over to Mai, flanking her on either side. Mai was embarrassed and furious at her brothers. Also their privacy had been invaded and abused by her Neanderthal-like older brothers.

"Mom, this is Vencel and Gaspar."

"Please accept my apology for my son's atrocious actions. I think they have been out in the field too long and lost what civil manners I taught them."

"There's no need to apologize for them Mrs. Bennett. I can understand their wanting to make certain that their little sister is safe." Vencel lifted her hand and pressed a kiss to the back of it.

Gaspar grinned and bent over to press a quick kiss to her cheek. "If we had a little sister, we would be overprotective, too."

"So which one of you boys is dating my daughter?"

Her mom looked back and forth from each twin to her daughter. Vencel held her hand while Gaspar's hand lay across the back on her neck in an obviously possessive action. Was he afraid that she would leave them? Mai could feel her cheeks flushing with heat. "Um, both."

She wrapped an arm around each man's waist.

"Good choice, cherry blossom." Her mom stepped forward and crooked a finger at each of her men. Vencel and Gaspar bent at the waist, and she kissed each of them on the cheek. "If you had only chosen one, your brothers would have ganged up on him. This way they don't have that option."

Vencel laughed. "I was about to put on a pot of coffee, Mrs. Bennett, would you like a cup?"

"That would be lovely. It was a long, silent drive up here, and I am parched. Neither of the boys wanted to stop. I have to say I'm glad that I insisted on joining them."

Mai crossed her arms over her chest and glared at her two overbearing older brothers. Each of them looked sheepish and remorseful. In turn, they each stepped up and shook Vencel and Gaspar's hands, apologizing for their behavior.

Marcario reached out and pulled Mai into his arms. "Oh, Maibee, don't be mad at me, okay? I'm sorry I embarrassed you in front of your boyfriend…er boyfriends."

"Me, too, blossom." Jelani kissed her on the temple. "I'm sorry I didn't ask first before jumping to conclusions."

"He does throw a hell of a punch though."

Mai looked up at Vencel and caught him rubbing his jaw.

"You punched him." Mai lunged at her brother with every intent of thumping him right on the chest. Gaspar grabbed her and wrapped his arms around her. "You know he's fine and trying to get extra sympathy from you."

"Vencel!"

He pretended not to hear her and ran into the kitchen with her brother fast on his heels. She looked back up at Gaspar. "I'm sorry they tried to barge in like that."

"Oh, *Angyalom*, don't worry about it. Both Vencel and I expected it was only a matter of time before they both came up here to make us answer for claiming you."

"How did you know?"

"Because, it's what we would have done in their position. Facing the possibility of your baby sister getting involved with one man is bad enough, but two might have been a bigger shock to them."

"I have to be honest, they took it very well. Much better than I expected them to."

"True, unless they feel the same way as Vencel and I do."

"All right that's enough. It's bad enough being caught by my mother and brothers in nothing but my boyfriend's T-shirt. I refuse to even think about my brother's sex life. Ewww, that's nasty."

Gaspar hugged her close and Mai enjoyed the peaceful feeling that washed over her. It felt as if a white light bathed them both. "*Szeretlek*, Gaspar."

"I love you, too, *Angyalom*. Where did you learn Hungarian?"

"I looked it up on the Internet."

"As much as I love to see you bounce around in my clothes. Why don't you go upstairs and change into something that isn't going to fire your brothers' tempers as much?"

Of course he didn't let her go until he kissed her soundly. Mai felt her insides go to mush and suggested that perhaps Gaspar could come upstairs with her for a quick moment.

"As tempting as it is to torture Vencel like that..." He brushed his lips against hers again. The light contact against her sensitized skin made her shiver. "I better go in there and give your brothers another target." He slipped his hand under her shirt and patted her bare bottom as she stepped on the bottom step before heading into the kitchen.

* * * *

It took every ounce of control in his body to not run out into the hallway and snuggle with his mate. Hearing her speak his native tongue and especially that word made him want to kick everyone out of the house and go back up stairs with her and his brother and make her repeat those words as they moved inside her.

Entertaining her mother was a pleasurable experience though. He poured coffee for everyone and set out some cream and sugar. Marcario and Jelani both glanced over at the doorway a couple times, as if waiting for their sister to enter with Gaspar.

"What is it you and your brother do up here, Vencel? Can you support my, Mai?"

"Yes, ma'am." He got out some bagels from the breadbox and the cream cheese and jam from the fridge as he spoke. "I have a successful construction company in Toronto. I'm getting away from the steel and glass condominiums and plan to build more ecofriendly housing up here. Gaspar recently changed his career path, but I've made enough to keep the three of us financially comfortable while he decides what path to take."

"You sit down."

Vencel looked over at Mai's mother, but she pointed at Jelani. In order to hide his grin, he turned and bent over and pulled the toaster out of the cupboard. Gaspar walked into the kitchen as Vencel started cutting bagels.

"Your brother said you've quit your job. Don't you think that you should have made alternate plans before doing that?"

Vencel could tell that Gaspar wasn't impressed with Jelani's blunt questioning, but if they had a sister in this situation, then he would imagine they'd have the same attitude.

"We have a friend who sits on an animal safety committee, and he asked me if I'd be interested in working for him." Vencel almost snorted at the way Gaspar worded the position Gordon offered them. Considering the help the pack had given them in taking care of the Hungarians, he understood his brother's need to help out.

"Both our hours will be flexible, giving us more time home with Mai."

Jelani took a sip of his coffee and nodded slightly. Marcario opened his mouth when Mai raced into the room. She looked panicked, putting both him and Gaspar on the defensive. "*Nyuszikam*, what is it?"

"I was afraid that you guys would be fighting again."

He sighed in relief and pressed a kiss to the top of her head. "I promise no more of that."

She smiled up at him and pressed her hand to his cheek. He could feel the love in her soul and by her smile knew she could feel the same emotions reflected back at her from his own. Their mate was perfect in every way and if it meant he had to be nice to her brothers, then that is exactly what he would do.

Szwewrlek, Nyuszikam. Her eyes widened in surprise.

You heard me in the hallway! Holy crap you hear me like this. Szwewrlek, Vencel.

There was a clearing of someone's throat and a nudge from his brother reminding Vencel that they weren't alone. Given the depth of Mai's blush, he knew she forgot as well. Her mother was giving them a grin, and both her brother's looked like they wanted to punch something. Probably him.

"I'm glad to hear that you both have plans, but what do you expect my Mai to do up here?"

"Mom!"

"It's all right, Mai." He turned to her mother. "Mai can do whatever she likes. If she wants to continue her web designs or take up spinning, we'll support any choice she makes."

"We're her partners, not her bosses." Gaspar went back to cooking up more bacon. The kitchen started to smell incredible, reminding Vencel how long it had been since they ate last. They both made certain that Mai ate a good breakfast. A fact that seemed to please her family. It looked like he and Gaspar weren't the only ones concerned by her lack of eating.

After breakfast, with everyone stuffed to capacity, he and Gaspar took them out on one of the easier hikes in the park. It weaved in and out of the trees, every once in a while they paused at a cliff edge that looked out over one of the parks' valleys. It looked like a sea of green dotted with the occasional bird. By the end of the day, he and Gaspar were getting along great with Marcario and Jelani. The four of them sauntered along the paths behind Mai and her mother. Mother and daughter were deep in conversation, but he deliberately didn't listen because he wanted Mai to feel that she had some time alone to spend with her mom.

Once back at the house, he barbequed steaks, while Mai and her mom made salads. They discussed hockey right up until the boys admitted that they were both Montreal Canadians fans. Mai came outside and threatened to thump all of them if they didn't stop fighting. The entire day was everything that Vencel didn't know he wanted. All his life, at least for the last sixty-five years, had been only him and his brother. It felt right to have family around again. He wasn't ready for pack life by any means, but a family he could live with.

There isn't any reason why we can't consider them pack.

Vencel frowned at Gaspar. *But they're human.*

So what? We turned our backs on the Hungarians and their rules. Perhaps Gordon has it right. Family is family no matter what your blood is.

I think that we make a pretty good family. A thrill ran through Vencel hearing his mate's voice in his head. There would never be any secrets, and she would never betray them.

Mai, my mate, we make an incredible family. Hopefully one day there will be more of us.

Do you think we should tell my family?

No, not yet. Let them get used to the idea of you being grown up and in a relationship with us. The rest can wait.

* * * *

Mai's nosy brothers and meddling mother finally headed home, but they weren't even out of the driveway when she started missing them.

"Don't cry, *Angyalom*. They'll come back again. We made certain that they realized they are welcome up here anytime."

"I spoke to Marcario about putting an addition on the house."

"That's so awesome! My brother is a great architect. I can't wait to see what he draws up for us."

Gaspar scooped her up into his arms and headed out the sliding doors in the kitchen.

"Where are we going?" Mai rested her head on his shoulder and closed her eyes. They could take her anywhere they wanted. She didn't feel the icy strains of panic teasing her from relaxing anymore. The warm summer sun shone down on the yarn, but there was enough of a breeze that it prevented the humidity from being to cloying.

"Oh, I think I'd like to pick up where we left off the other day."

Mai lifted her head and frowned at him. "I'm not running through the forest again. That didn't end well."

"No, not that one."

She looked over his shoulder and watched Vencel emerge from the house. He carried a bunch of blankets over one arm. As he got close to him, she noticed him smelling the air as well. "Is everything okay?"

"Everything is simply perfect."

Moments later the blankets were all laid out and the three of them lay naked in the sunshine. Mai reclined back on her elbows between the two of them. Vencel rubbed sunscreen into her arms as Gaspar did the same to her legs. She felt like a goddess being worshiped in the sun. Nothing could be better than this. "What about the two of you?"

"We don't burn." Gaspar stroked up her inner thigh, his fingers brushing her curls ever so slightly. She let her legs fall open, inviting him to touch her wherever he liked.

"But we aren't going to take a chance with your delicate skin." Vencel held her hands over her head and leaned down to kiss her. His tongue flicked at the seam of her lips, but Mai didn't open them. Instead, she lifted her head slightly and nipped at his bottom lip. Catching it between her teeth, she tugged slightly before letting go. Vencel growled low in his chest and swooped down, claiming her mouth for his own. He kissed her as if he was afraid he might lose her. Silly man, didn't he realize that he had tattooed himself on her soul? Both he and his brother would never leave her, and if she wanted to travel, then they would go with her.

Mai could feel their emotions surrounding her, wrapping her in a protective cocoon. It didn't feel claustrophobic. Instead, it was like sand being poured in a jar filled with colorful marbles. They supported her, but she still was in control of herself. The three of them were like silk threads in a tapestry. Each strong on their own, but woven together they became as strong as steel and incredibly beautiful.

They made love under the sun, each man taking turns with her body and trying to keep up with her demands.

"I love you both so much."

"*Szeretlek*, mate." She felt the words vibrate under her cheek where it rested on his chest. Vencel pressed a kiss against the back on her neck and wrapped an arm around her waist. "We love you, too. You're our pack and family, and we will make certain you'll never have to fear anything again."

THE END

WWW.CORINNEDAVIES.COM

ABOUT THE AUTHOR

Corinne Davies reads anything she can get her hands on, from the side of a cereal box to a historical book on the Riflemen during the Napoleonic wars. By day, she is a full-time wife and mother and works in the wine industry. At night, she avoids such mundane tasks as housework and laundry by creating her own worlds where mythology comes to life—worlds in which you are just as likely to be living next door to an ancient deity as finding a mystic treasure in the attic.

Also by Corinne Davies

Ménage Amour: *Believing is Seeing*
Ménage and More: Sequel to *Believing is Seeing: Believing is Trusting*
Siren Classic: *Haunted Hearts*
Ménage Amour: *Steam Powered Passion*

Available at
BOOKSTRAND.COM

Siren Publishing, Inc.
www.SirenPublishing.com